W9-ASA-768

Just a Friendly Conversation

Clint stepped into the room, listened, and heard the even breathing of a sleeping man. He waited for his eyes to adjust to the darkness in the room. When he could make out the man in the bed, he moved to it and pressed the gun to the sleeping man's forehead. The man woke up immediately.

"Move and I'll blow your brains out, Cooper," Clint said.

The man stayed still.

"Where's my wife?"

"Upstairs," Clint said. "She's all right." He saw the man's gun on the night table next to the bed. He grabbed it and tucked it into his belt.

"Light the lamp," he told Cooper. "We're going to have a talk."

"About what?"

"Light it," Clint said. "We'll get to that."

He allowed the man to sit up nervously and light the lamp by the bed.

"Now what?" Cooper asked.

"Now you tell me who you work for."

"If I do that," Cooper said, "I'm dead."

"If you don't tell me, I'll kill you right now," Clint told him. "Your choice."

DON'T MISS THESE
ALL-ACTION WESTERN SERIES
FROM THE BERKLEY PUBLISHING GROUP

THE GUNSMITH by J. R. Roberts
Clint Adams was a legend among lawmen, outlaws, and ladies.
They called him . . . the Gunsmith.

LONGARM by Tabor Evans
The popular long-running series about Deputy U.S. Marshal
Custis Long—his life, his loves, his fight for justice.

SLOCUM by Jake Logan
Today's longest-running action Western. John Slocum rides a
deadly trail of hot blood and cold steel.

BUSHWHACKERS by B. J. Lanagan
An action-packed series by the creators of Longarm! The rous-
ing adventures of the most brutal gang of cutthroats ever
assembled—Quantrill's Raiders.

DIAMONDBACK by Guy Brewer
Dex Yancey is Diamondback, a Southern gentleman turned con
man when his brother cheats him out of the family fortune.
Ladies love him. Gamblers hate him. But nobody pulls one over
on Dex . . .

WILDGUN by Jack Hanson
The blazing adventures of mountain man Will Barlow—from
the creators of Longarm!

TEXAS TRACKER by Tom Calhoun
J.T. Law: the most relentless—and dangerous—manhunter in
all Texas. Where sheriffs and posses fail, he's the best man to
bring in the most vicious outlaws—for a price.

THE GUNSMITH

384

LOUISIANA STALKER

J. R. ROBERTS

JOVE BOOKS, NEW YORK

THE BERKLEY PUBLISHING GROUP
Published by the Penguin Group
Penguin Group (USA) LLC
375 Hudson Street, New York, New York 10014, USA

USA • Canada • UK • Ireland • Australia • New Zealand • India • South Africa • China

penguin.com.

A Penguin Random House Company

LOUISIANA STALKER

A Jove Book / published by arrangement with the author

Copyright © 2013 by Robert J. Randisi.
Penguin supports copyright. Copyright fuels creativity, encourages diverse voices,
promotes free speech, and creates a vibrant culture. Thank you for having an authorized
edition of this book and for complying with copyright laws by not reproducing, scanning,
or distributing any part of it in any form without permission. You are supporting writers
and allowing Penguin to continue to publish books for every reader.

JOVE® is a registered trademark of Penguin Group (USA) LLC.
The "J" design is a trademark of Penguin Group (USA) LLC.

For information, address: The Berkley Publishing Group,
a division of Penguin Group (USA),
375 Hudson Street, New York, New York 10014.

ISBN: 978-0-515-15392-7

PUBLISHING HISTORY
Jove mass-market edition / December 2013

PRINTED IN THE UNITED STATES OF AMERICA

10 9 8 7 6 5 4 3 2 1

Cover illustration by Sergio Giovine.

This is a work of fiction. Names, characters, places, and incidents either are the product
of the author's imagination or are used fictitiously, and any resemblance to actual persons,
living or dead, business establishments, events, or locales is entirely coincidental.
The publisher does not have any control over and does not assume any responsibility for
author or third-party websites or their content.

If you purchased this book without a cover, you should be aware that this book is
stolen property. It was reported as "unsold and destroyed" to the publisher, and neither
the author nor the publisher has received any payment for this "stripped book."

ONE

As Clint Adams rode from Texas into Louisiana, he looked behind him again. Still there, and still not hiding. It had been weeks now that this tail had been on him, but never any closer. Just a figure off in the distance, sometimes sitting a horse, sometimes just standing, watching.

It had been weeks, states, and many miles . . .

It had begun in Arizona, the first time he'd noticed the man—and he thought it was a man—on his back trail. Not tracking, because that implied trying to catch someone. This rider kept the same distance between them at all times.

He stopped in Jennings, Arizona, and waited, but the man never rode in. Days later when he left Jennings, there he was again, still the same distance away.

All the way to New Mexico . . .

New Mexico was much the same, so he decided to take a more active pose. He tried to wait for the man to catch up, but he never did. He attempted to circle around behind him, but the man was too good for that. Too good for Clint to be comfortable about it.

In a town called Runnels, New Mexico, he bought a

high-powered spyglass. Outside of town he picked out a high
bluff, got comfortable on his belly, and watched through the
spyglass. It was as if the man knew the range of the piece.
Clint could see he was wearing trail clothes, a holster and
handgun. He was not carrying a rifle. Clint could not see the
man's face.

He tried again several times over the next few days, but
the range never improved. He was never close enough to make
out the man's features.

His tail seemed very content with the way things were.
Maybe he was just trying to get under the Gunsmith's skin.

He was succeeding . . .

As he crossed into Louisiana from Texas, Clint wondered
how long the man was going to keep this up. At some point
he must have intended to close the distance, either to take a
shot or to make some sort of contact.

He wondered how much patience this mysterious man
could possibly have.

He noticed something new the next time he used the spyglass.
A cigar in the man's mouth. He was a smoker. That was new.
Still not holding a rifle. Still no apparent interest in doing
anything but watching.

Clint could have taken some sort of evasive action. He
could have outrun the man with Eclipse, gotten away from
him. After that, the man would have had to actually track
him, and Clint could have avoided him.

But he decided not to.

He decided to let the man follow him all he wanted. He
could have taken a shot at any time, and didn't. If he'd wanted
to kill him, he could have tried by now. So let the man follow
for as long as he wanted to. At some point he'd either quit, or
make contact.

He stopped trying to get a look at him with the spyglass.

Every so often he'd turn his head and look back, but that was all he was giving the man now.

He rode on, Baton Rouge his ultimate destination.

The man following the Gunsmith looked on with satisfaction. Adams had put away his spyglass and stopped trying to get a look at his face. That was good. For a while he thought he was getting under Adams's skin, but now the Gunsmith seemed to have accepted him.

It took long enough.

TWO

Clint had not been to Baton Rouge in some time. Normally, if he was in Louisiana, it was to spend some time in New Orleans. Baton Rouge, though, was like a smaller version of New Orleans. There were beautiful homes, thriving businesses, and a lively riverfront.

He rode into town, realizing that it was more city than anything else these days. It was late afternoon and the streets were still teeming with people.

Clint decided to put his tail out of his mind. He intended to be in Baton Rouge for a while. If the man eventually decided to come in, that was his business. He directed Eclipse down the main street until he came to a livery stable.

"Things have changed around here since my last visit," he told the hostler.

"How long's it been?" the man asked.

"Can't remember," Clint said. "I usually go to New Orleans."

"Hell," the man said, "we got everythin' New Orleans got." He stroked Eclipse's neck. "Ain't got no horses like this around here, though. How you doin', *cher?*" He rubbed Eclipse's nose, and the big gelding withstood it.

"You got a way with horses," Clint said. "He's not usually that patient with people touching him."

"You got a beautiful animal here," the man said. "They's need to be touched, and talked to."

"Well," Clint said, "I guess I'm putting him in good hands."

"You can bet on that," the man said. "How long you stayin'?"

"A few days, at least," Clint said. "I want to see all that Baton Rouge has to offer."

"You have yourself a good time, and don't worry none about this here big fella," the man said. "He is in good hands."

Clint retrieved his saddlebags and rifle from his saddle, then gave Eclipse an affectionate slap on the rump as the man walked the big gelding into the stable.

With his saddlebags over his shoulder and his rifle in his left hand—leaving his right hand free—he started back up the street, looking for a likely hotel. He didn't want the best place in town, but neither did he want a dive. He found the place he wanted after a couple of blocks, on Government Street. It was called the Cajun House and had an appearance that made one think of mint juleps on the veranda. It was small, well appointed, looked to have been built just over the past few years, but then a lot of the buildings had that look.

He entered the lobby and was greeted effusively by a young, well-dressed desk clerk.

"Good afternoon, sir," the man said, "welcome to the Cajun House. What can I do for you on this fine day?"

"I'd like a room, please."

"Of course, of course," the young man said. "Please sign the register. We have a few rooms left."

"Anything overlooking the street?"

"Let me see." The man turned, examining his keys. "Why yes, I do have something." He turned with the key, reversed the register so he could read the name. "Mr. . . . . Adams. Clint Adams?"

"That's right."

"Well . . . it's a pleasure to have someone of your stature staying with us, sir."

"Thank you. My key?"

"Yes, sir," the man said, suddenly noticing that he was still holding the key. He handed it over. "Room six, gives you a nice view of Government Street, sir."

"Thanks."

"Is there anything else I can do for you?"

"Yes," Clint said, "don't hit the street with the word that I'm staying here as soon as I go upstairs."

"Um, well, no, sir," the young man said, "I wouldn't, uh, do that."

"Good," Clint said, "because that wouldn't make me very happy."

"No, sir," the man said.

Clint smiled, then took the stairs to the second floor.

When he got to his room, he leaned the rifle against the wall in a corner and dropped his saddlebags on the bed. He walked to the window and looked out. The clerk was right—he had a good view of the street, both ways. At the moment it was alive with people, probably most of them returning home from work.

Clint needed a bath and a good suit of clothes. The places he was planning to visit would require a certain manner of dress. He should have told the clerk to draw him a bath. He'd have to go back down and do that. Maybe the young man could also assist him in getting a shave and a haircut . . .

"Certainly, sir," the clerk said when Clint reappeared at the lobby desk. "I can have the barber come in and take care of that for you before or after your bath."

"Let's do it before, thanks."

"Yes, sir."

"How soon can he be here?"

"No time at all, sir," the clerk said. "I'll have him come directly to your room."

"Okay, thanks," Clint said. "After all of that, I have to go out and find a good suit."

"I can help you with that, as well, sir."

"Oh? How so?"

"I can also have the tailor come to your room. He can take your measurements and have your suit ready for you by tomorrow."

"That soon?"

"Oh, yes, sir," the clerk said, especially after the tailor realizes you're a, uh, special guest."

"Special guest?" Clint said. "Does that mean my room is cheaper?"

The clerk looked puzzled, then he laughed and said, "Oh, sir, that's a good one."

THREE

The tailor appeared at the door just as the barber was finishing up. While Clint opened the door, the barber was very busily collecting Clint's hair from the floor and putting it in a bag.

"You going to sell that?" Clint asked him.

The man looked at him guiltily.

"That's okay," Clint told him. "Just make sure you get a good price."

"Yes, sir," the barber said. "Thank you."

"When you get to the lobby, ask the clerk to draw a bath for me, will you?" Clint said.

"Yes, sir."

The barber left and Clint closed the door behind him. As he turned around, the tailor was taking his tape measure from around his neck. He was a meek-looking man with a potbelly and very little hair on his head.

"One suit, sir?" he asked.

"Yes," Clint said, "just one. And you can have it done by tomorrow?"

"For you, sir, of course."

"Good."

Even while the tailor was taking measurements, Clint's

gun was never out of reach. The man was very efficient and was finished quickly.

"I'll have the suit here tomorrow afternoon, sir," he said as Clint let him out.

"That'll be great," Clint said. "Thanks."

He closed the door, collected some fresh clothes and his gun, and went down to take his bath.

When he left the hotel, he felt fresh and clean, newly shorn and shaven. The only thing remaining was to fill the hunger in his belly with a steak.

He had his choice of good restaurants, so he simply stopped into the closest one. Before long he had a steak dinner in front of him, with potatoes and onions, green beans, and coffee. The place was crowded, but he was able to get a table in the back. From there he could see everyone, and no one seemed particularly interested in him. If his tail was in the room, he wasn't being obvious about watching him. That meant it wasn't likely he was there, because up to now he'd been very obvious.

The steak was excellent, prepared just right, and the coffee was as strong as he liked it. Afterward he topped it off with pie—apple, because they didn't have peach—and he enjoyed that, too.

When he left the restaurant, it was dusk. The street was a damn sight less busy than it had been when he went in. It was a perfect time to walk the streets, get acquainted with Baton Rouge, and maybe stop in on the local law.

Storefronts were closed and locked up, but Clint could see that Baton Rouge had every kind of business you could possibly think of. Restaurants were lit up and open, all busy. He also passed a few bawdy houses, where the women were right outside on the balconies, showing off their wares, which were—in many cases—not only lovely, but considerable. Made him have second thoughts about his rule not to pay for sex—almost.

However, even given everything the town had to offer, he still found it lacking the charm of New Orleans's French Quarter.

He passed both the Baton Rouge Police Department, and later the sheriff's office. He made the decision to check in with the sheriff, and not the police. He still preferred the sheriff's and marshal's offices to the modern police departments that were moving in on the Western towns of late.

He stopped in front of the sheriff's office and read the shingle there: BEAUREGUARD LEBLANC, SHERIFF. Quite a name, he thought as he knocked and then entered.

While the outside of the sheriff's office was weathered, obviously one of the older buildings in town, the inside had recently been redone. The walls had a fresh coat of paint, the hardwood floors seemed to have been buffed, and the desk the sheriff was sitting behind was gleaming cherry wood, and huge.

"Evenin', sir," the lawman said, looking up at Clint. "What can I do for you?"

"Sheriff LeBlanc?"

"That's what it says on the shingle," the man replied, "but around here most folks just call me Beau."

The sheriff seemed as new as the desk. He was barely thirty, and though the young man was seated, Clint could tell he was tall, with broad shoulders and a firm jaw. He had obviously not been wearing a badge long enough to become world-weary about it.

"I've just ridden into town and thought I'd check in with you," Clint said.

"Well, that's real nice of you," LeBlanc said, "but is there any particular reason you felt the need to do that?"

"My name is Clint Adams."

For a moment he thought the man didn't recognize the name. He hated the thought that he might have to elaborate, but recognition finally dawned on the younger man's face and he pointed his finger at Clint and said, "The Gunsmith, right?"

"That's right."

LeBlanc immediately stood, and Clint could see he was not wearing a gun. The man stuck his hand out and said, "Well, this is a great pleasure, sir, a great pleasure."

Clint took the man's hand, allowed him to pump his hand vigorously.

"What brings a legend to Baton Rouge?" LeBlanc asked.

"Haven't been here in a while," Clint said, retrieving his hand. "Thought I'd check the town out and see how it had grown."

"Well," LeBlanc said, "I'm sure you've seen that we've grown by leaps and bounds."

"Yes, I can see that," Clint said.

"And I don't think you'll have any worries while you're here," the sheriff said.

"How do you mean?"

"We've come about as far from the Old West as you could get," LeBlanc said. "You won't have anyone trying to push you into a gunfight on the street. We just don't do that here."

Clint had already found that to be true every time he went to New Orleans, but he was sure that challenging another man to a duel was still in fashion. Especially among the well-to-do denizens of the Garden District.

"That's good to hear," he said.

"And I appreciate you coming in to let me know you're here," LeBlanc said. "Perhaps we can even have a drink together at some point?"

"That'd be fine with me," Clint said.

"Where are you staying?"

"The Cajun House."

"A fine establishment," LeBlanc said. "Will you be gambling while here? We can offer you every form of games of chance."

"I might be persuaded to play some poker," Clint admitted.

"Excellent," LeBlanc said. "I hope you'll enjoy your stay. Oh, uh, and how long would you be staying?"

"Not sure," Clint said. "Probably a few days."

"Hopefully more," LeBlanc said with a wide smile. "And while you're here, please let me know if I can do anything for you."

"I'll do that."

FOUR

Clint left the sheriff's office, wondering if Baton Rouge had become the kind of place where a man like Beau LeBlanc could be an effective lawman.

The mention of gambling had whet his appetite for some poker, but he decided to wait until the next day. He wanted to get a good night's sleep, and that new suit, before he started touring the gambling houses.

He returned to his hotel, exchanged a friendly nod with the young desk clerk, and went to his room.

He moved his boots and sat on the firm mattress. It struck him how young both the desk clerk and the lawman had been. Thankfully, his waiter had been a bit older. He was afraid the men in this town were going to make him feel older than he was.

He read some Dickens, then doused the lamp, removed his clothes, and turned in for the night.

He awoke the next morning refreshed. He decided to try the Cajun House's own restaurant for breakfast, thinking that maybe his new suit would arrive by the time he was done.

He ordered steak and eggs, which were prepared perfectly. The coffee could have been stronger, but was acceptable. The waiter told him he could charge the meal to his room, and pay for it all together when he checked out.

"That's very civilized," Clint said. "Thank you."

"Yes, sir."

Clint left two bits on the table for the waiter and went out to the lobby.

"Mr. Adams?" the clerk called.

He turned and looked at the man. "Yes?"

"I have a message for you."

"Is that so?" He approached the desk. "From who?"

"I don't know," the man said. "It was left on the desk while I was . . . away."

He handed Clint an envelope, which was sealed.

"Thank you."

"Yes, sir."

Clint carried the envelope with him away from the desk. He debated whether he should read the message there in the lobby, or in his room. He decided to open it right there. He sat on a sofa against one wall and opened the envelope. Immediately, a perfume smell rose from inside. The message was obviously from a lady, but who knew he was there?

He unfolded the perfumed note and read it. It was an invitation to have supper with a woman named Capucine Devereaux. He didn't know the woman, but the perfume smelled expensive. The invitation was for 8 p.m. at a restaurant called Chez Louis.

He stood and walked back to the front desk.

"What's your name?" he asked the clerk.

"Ronald, sir."

"Well, Ronald, what can you tell me about a restaurant called Chez Louis?"

"Ah"—the young man's eyes lit up—"one of the best restaurants in Baton Rouge, sir. But also, I'm afraid, one of the most expensive."

"I see," Clint said, "and do you know anything about the name 'Devereaux'?"

"One of the finest families not in only Baton Rouge, but in all of Louisiana."

"A rich family?"

"Oh, yes."

"I see."

"Is that who the note was from, sir?" Ronald asked. "The Devereaux family?"

"Thanks for the information, Ronald."

"If the Devereaux family has summoned you, sir, you had best respond."

"Is that so?"

"Simon Devereaux is a very powerful man."

"Then why would he need me?"

"You're the Gunsmith," Ronald said as if that alone should explain it.

"I know who I am," Clint said. "Okay, thanks."

There was no way for him to acknowledge the invitation. He assumed that Capucine Devereaux, whoever she was—daughter? wife?—would wait for him at Chez Louis, in the hope that he would accept the invitation.

He had all day to decide.

Clint's new suit was delivered to him before he left the hotel. He had the tailor hang it in his room. Then he waited for the saloons and gambling houses to open. He visited six of them, nursed half a beer in each, picking out the ones he would definitely visit later that night, while wearing his new suit, to do his gambling.

During the course of the day he thought about the note in his pocket. How had Capucine Devereaux known that he was in Baton Rouge, and at what hotel he was staying? There were only two people who knew that, Ronald the clerk and Sheriff LeBlanc. What motive could either of them have for telling her? He could find out the answers to all those questions by accepting the lady's invitation to supper. And he could do that while wearing his new suit. Of course, he'd also bring along his little friend, the Colt New Line, which would fit comfortably beneath his jacket without being seen.

He didn't mind accepting a blind invitation like this, but he'd never think of doing it unarmed.

In fact, the Gunsmith never did anything unarmed. Even in bed—with or without a woman—his gun was always within arm's reach.

He finished the last of his beer in the sixth gambling house—once again drinking only half—and went back to his hotel to get ready for his supper date.

FIVE

Resplendent in his new suit, with the Colt New Line comfortably nestled in the small of his back, Clint left the Cajun House and flagged down a cab.

"Do you know where Chez Louis is?" he asked the driver—again, a young man, like the clerk and the lawman.

"Everybody knows where Chez Louis is," the driver said.

"Okay, well, take me there, then."

"Hop in, sir."

It was a mild night, so driving in the open-air cab was a pleasure. There were a lot more lights at night in Baton Rouge than there had been the last time he was there. He didn't know who the mayor of the city was, but he was apparently doing a hell of a job.

The cab pulled to a stop in front of Chez Louis, which was not lit up. It had a classy, dark front with a large, stenciled plate glass window.

"Here ya go," the driver said. "Hope you got a fat wallet."

"I'm a guest," Clint said, paying the man his fare.

"Lucky you! Wish I had somebody who'd buy me supper here."

"Maybe you will someday."

"Want me to wait for you and take you back?"

"Won't be going right back," Clint said. "I'll be stopping to do some gambling first."

"I can come back and get ya," the man said. "I know all the places a gent like you should gamble."

"Why not? Come back in an hour. I should be finished by then."

"If you're not, I'll just wait," the young man said.

"What's your name?"

"Henri, sir."

"Well, Henri," Clint said, handing the young man some extra money, "maybe this will make it worth your while to wait."

"Yes, sir!"

Clint left his jacket unbuttoned—easier access to the Colt—and entered the restaurant.

Inside was dark, mostly burgundy leather, with an occasional gleam of gold. The tuxedoed maître d' greeted him. He was glad to see that the man was middle-aged.

"Good evening, sir. Can I help you?"

"Yes, I'm meeting Capucine Devereaux here."

"Ah, then you would be Mr. Adams?"

"That's right."

"Excellent," the man said. "How wonderful to have you with us, sir. Please follow me."

The man led Clint through the crowded restaurant to a table in the back that seemed to have more room around it than the others, as if other tables near it had been removed.

He led Clint to a table where two ladies were seated, one slightly older than the other, but both beautiful. He assumed the older woman—in her thirties—was Capucine Devereaux, since she seemed to be dressed in the more expensive finery. The other woman was not yet thirty.

"Mrs. Devereaux," the maître d' said, bowing slightly at the waist, "your guest has arrived."

"Thank you, André."

André looked at Clint.

"Mr. Adams, Mrs. Devereaux."

"Ma'am," Clint said, "it's a pleasure to meet you."

"Please, Mr. Adams," Capucine Devereaux said, "take a seat."

But Clint, whose hat was in his hands at this point, did not sit. Instead, he looked at the younger woman.

"Ah," Mrs. Devereaux said, "I see we have a man with manners. Mr. Adams, please meet my assistant, Jeannie Bartlett."

"Miss Bartlett."

"Mr. Adams."

"And now will you sit?" Mrs. Devereaux asked.

"Happy to."

"Your waiter will be Pierre," André said. "I will send him right over."

"Send him with brandy, please, André."

"Yes, madame."

André withdrew and Mrs. Devereaux looked across the table at Clint. The other woman, Jeannie, kept her eyes down.

"I am very glad you decided to accept my invitation, Mr. Adams," Mrs. Devereaux said, "especially since you have no idea who I am."

"I asked around, Mrs. Devereaux."

"And you learned something that made you come?"

"I did," he said. "I learned that this is one of the best restaurants in Baton Rouge."

"Indeed," she said, "as far as I am concerned, it is the best, although my husband prefers the local fare to French."

"I thought this was local."

"This is a French restaurant," she informed him, "but not a Cajun restaurant."

"Ah."

"Although if you'd prefer something Cajun, I'm sure the chef could handle it for you."

"No, that's fine," he said.

Mrs. Devereaux was a redhead, with pale skin and just the requisite dusting of freckles being a redhead required. She wore a jade green gown that was low cut, revealing an impressive expanse of pale cleavage.

Jeannie Bartlett had dark hair, with pale skin and very large brown eyes—when he could see them. She was slender, and very pretty. One or both of them smelled very sweet.

"I'm sure you are wondering why I invited you—a perfect stranger—to have supper with me."

"That's one of the things I'm wondering about," he said.

"Would you mind if we got to all your questions after supper?" she asked.

"I happen to be very hungry," he said, "so no, I don't mind, at all."

SIX

They drank brandy before supper, and wine with it. Clint's preference was beer, but he knew good liquor and wine when he tasted it. Mrs. Devereaux was ordering the best.

She did, however, allow Clint to order supper for himself, and he found a steak dish on the menu. He chose steak au poivre—steak seasoned with black pepper and adorned with a brandy and cream sauce. The meat was cooked to perfection, although he might have preferred it without the sauce. He did, however, enjoy all the accompanying vegetables.

Mrs. Devereaux explained throughout dinner that her husband was in the shipping business, and made good use of the Mississippi River, shipping items from Louisiana to Minnesota, and points in between. Also, the Devereaux family had a long history in Louisiana, had a home in Baton Rouge, a home in New Orleans, and a plantation on the bayou.

"I do a lot of charity work," she went on, "and Jeannie is invaluable to me in keeping everything running smoothly. Are you enjoying your supper?"

"Very much."

Both women had ordered seafood. Jeannie was eating filet of sole Veronique, while Mrs. Devereaux had ordered salmon en croute.

"Will you allow me to at least order dessert for us?" she asked.

"Of course."

She proceeded to order a raspberry brûlée for all of them, as well as coffee—French roast, of course.

After dessert, Mrs. Devereaux ordered more coffee and then said to Clint, "Perhaps we should get down to business?"

"Is that what this is about? Business?"

"Well . . . perhaps," she said.

"First," he said, "my questions."

"Ah, yes," she replied, "I did say I'd answer them, didn't I?"

"Yes, you did."

"Very well." She slid her fingertips lightly across the slopes of her breasts. "Ask away."

Clint looked at Jeannie, who lowered her eyes once again.

"How did you know I was in Baton Rouge? And at the Cajun House?"

"That is an easy question," she said. "Sheriff LeBlanc sent word to me that you had visited him, and told me where you were staying."

"Why did he do that?"

"Because he knew I needed a man," she said, "a man capable of boldness."

"And you assumed I was such a man?"

"I am aware of your reputation, Mr. Adams," she said, "as the Gunsmith. But I am also aware that reputations can be . . . shall we say, inflated?"

"That's more than most people seem to be aware of," he said.

"I thought I would invite you dinner and find out for myself if you are the man I need."

"The man you need for what?"

"A job."

"I'm not for hire."

"A favor, then."

He hesitated, then said, "I have been known to do favors . . . for friends."

"What about ladies in distress?" she asked.

"Then this job you need done," he said, "is for you, not for your husband?"

"My husband doesn't know anything about it," she said. "And I desire to keep it that way."

"Is that possible?" he asked. "As powerful a man as he appears to be? Can you keep things from him?"

"I believe I can," she said, "though not many can say the same."

He studied her across the table.

"You're not French, are you?"

"No," she said, "and neither am I Cajun."

"I'd guess . . . Irish."

She smiled.

"Very good. I am only a lady because my husband married me, Mr. Adams."

"Clint," he said, "please."

"Clint," she said. "And my friends call me . . . Cappy. Also you obviously realize by now that Capucine is not my real name."

"Not very Irish, is it?"

"No."

"Ma'am—" Jeannie started.

"It's all right, Jeannie," Capucine said, "if Mr. Adams is to do what I ask of him, he must know everything." She looked at Clint. "Isn't that true?"

He smiled across the table at her and said, "That would be extremely helpful, Cappy."

SEVEN

"How does the sheriff know you need someone?"

"Well, I told him."

"And did you tell him what you need this bold man to do?" he asked

"I did not," she said. "I did think, at one time, that perhaps he was the man to help me, but I decided that he was not."

"Because what you want is illegal?"

"Because I did not think he was capable of what I needed," she said. "But I thought he might know a man who was."

"And did he?"

She hesitated, then said, "He did know a man, but it did not work out."

"And what happened to that man?"

"He has become part of the problem."

"Ah . . ."

The waiter came over with a fresh pot of coffee, and they fell silent until he had withdrawn.

"So he told you he'd be on the lookout for someone else?" Clint asked.

"No," she said, "I did not trust his judgment after . . . that, but he sent me a note telling me that the Gunsmith was in

Baton Rouge. Naturally, I acted immediately and had Jeannie deliver my note."

"And here we are," Clint said.

"Yes, here we are," she said. "All three of us."

"And Jeannie," Clint said, "she knows all the details?"

"Oh, yes," Capucine said, "I trust her implicitly—with all the sordid details."

"The details are sordid, are they?"

"I'm afraid so."

"And you plan to reveal them to me here?"

"No," she said, "not here. Someplace more private. I asked you here simply to meet you, spend time with you, and then decide if I would tell you the story. And see if you would agree to listen to it."

"What if you tell me the whole story and I don't agree to help?"

"I think you will agree."

"But if I don't, I'll know all the details."

"And that will make four of us," she said. "I'm afraid I'll have to take that chance."

Clint picked up his cup and drank from it, then refilled it himself. He offered the coffeepot to both ladies, who refused.

"All right," he said, "I'll listen. Where?"

"I have a pied-à-terre in the Garden District."

Clint looked at Jeannie, who happened to be looking at him at the moment.

"A small, private set of rooms that no one knows about," she offered.

"Ah."

"Jeannie knows where it is," Capucine said. "She will tell you when you escort her home this evening."

"Oh? Will I be escorting her home tonight?"

"You will," Capucine said. "I have another stop to make."

"Is that wise?" he asked. "I mean, for you to go out somewhere alone?"

"I won't be alone," she said. "My driver will be with me,

and as a matter of fact, I am going to be meeting my husband for drinks."

"Ah," he said, "I see."

"So," she said "if you will join me tomorrow afternoon, I will send a carriage for you. I will pay the check while you and Jeannie start for home."

Clint had the distinct feeling he and the assistant had just been dismissed.

They found Henri waiting for them out front with his cab. He hopped down to be a gentleman and help Jeannie up into his vehicle.

"Where are we headed?" he asked Clint.

"The Cajun House," Jeannie said.

"That's my hotel," he told her.

She looked him in the eye, something she had not done all during the meal. In fact, now that they were away from Capucine Devereaux, her entire demeanor seemed to have changed.

"I know that," she said. "I'm not quite ready to return home yet. I thought we could have a private drink at your hotel. Is that all right?"

"Uh, that's fine," Clint said. He looked at Henri. "You heard the lady."

"The Cajun House," Henri said. "Comin' up." But instead of climbing onto his perch, he lowered his voice and asked, "And how was the meal?"

"It was fine," Clint said, "but give me a good old American-cooked steak every time."

"Ah," Henri said, "that can be arranged."

Henri got himself situated and Clint climbed into the back of the cab, sitting across from Jeannie.

"Why don't you sit over here next to me?" she suggested.

Yes, he thought, shifting his seat, definitely a different demeanor.

EIGHT

They rode to the Cajun House with Jeannie's hip pressed firmly against Clint's. He could feel the warmth of her through their clothes.

"I'll bet you could tell me what your employer's problem is right now," he said.

"If I wanted to," she said.

"And?"

"I don't want to," she answered airily. "That's her business."

"Isn't her business also your business?" he asked. "I mean, isn't that what being an assistant is all about?"

"Well, yeah, it is," she said, and then added, "during business hours."

"And when exactly did business hours end for you?" he asked her.

She put her hand on his arm and squeezed.

"The moment we left Chez Louis."

"By the way . . ."

"Yes?"

"Is there actually a Louis?" he asked.

She laughed, and didn't answer.

* * *

As they entered the hotel lobby, Clint started for the bar, but Jeannie—who had linked her arm in his—yanked him back forcefully.

"The bar is this way," he told her.

"Yes," she said, "I know, but . . . isn't your room this way?"

"My room?"

"Yes," she said, her eyes wide and innocent, "can't we have a drink in your room?"

"My room is nothing fancy," he warned her. "Certainly not what you're used to."

"As long as it has a drink," she said, and then added, "and a bed."

Her intention was clear, and while he had no objection to it, he felt as if he was in the company of a third woman, one who was not at supper, at all.

"Just let me stop at the front desk."

"All right." Reluctantly, she released his arm.

He went to the front desk, where the young desk clerk was smiling at him.

"I'll need a bottle of brandy and two glasses in my room right away."

"Yessir!" the young man said. "Comin' up."

Clint started away, then stopped and said, "Whoever brings them up, if I don't answer the door, tell them to just leave them outside the room."

"Yes, sir!" the young man said with an even bigger smile.

"And wipe that smile off your face!"

Clint walked to Jeannie, took her arm, and led her up the stairs.

After Clint and Jeannie left, Capucine signed for the meal—which her husband would pay for later—and stepped outside. Her driver was waiting with her carriage. He opened the door for her, and she stepped into the enclosed car.

"Where to, ma'am?" he asked.

"The Club," she told him.

"Yes, ma'am."

He drove her to the Club, stopping at a rear door, as he usually did when he took her there. He held the carriage door open for her, helped her out, then opened the back door of the building for her.

"Shall I wait, ma'am?" he asked.

"No, Eric," she said, "I'll be getting a ride home later."

"Yes, ma'am."

He closed the door behind her, climbed aboard the carriage, and drove away.

Once she and Clint were in his room, Jeannie said, "Seems to me a man like you would have stayed at the Palace, or some such place."

"Much too fancy for me," he told her.

"So you're not a fancy man?"

"I'm not."

"So why the suit?"

"I may not stay at the Palace," Clint said, "but I'll go there to gamble."

"And dress the part, huh?"

"I wouldn't want to get turned away at the door," he said.

Jeannie was wearing a wrap, which she now took off and set aside on a chair. The sweet scent he'd smelled at the restaurant was in the air, so he now knew it was her, and not Capucine.

"Well?" she asked.

"Well what?"

"Will you undress me," she asked, raising her hands above her head, "or would you like to watch while I do it myself?"

NINE

"Why are you doing this?" Clint asked Jeannie.

She put her hands on her hips.

"Do you always ask a girl why she wants to sleep with you?" she asked.

"Not always."

"Why now?"

"I'm curious."

Jeannie hesitated a moment, then lifted her chin and said, "Well, she's eventually going to get you into bed. I just want to beat her to it."

"I see."

"Did you think it was because I was in love with you?" she asked.

"No," he said, "I didn't think that. But what makes you think she'll eventually get me into bed?"

"It's what she does," Jeannie said, "and I've never known of a man who told her no."

"I might be the first."

She laughed.

"You accepted her invitation to supper," she said, "and you agreed to meet with her tomorrow in private. And suddenly you're going to start saying no?" She raised her arms again. "Now, what's it going to be? You or me?"

He studied her for a long moment, then said, "I'll do it."

The man at the table stood up as Capucine entered the room and said, "Hello, darling."

"Oh, do sit down," she told him, gesturing with her hand then sitting across from him.

He did as he was told.

"Can I get you a drink?"

"Pour me a brandy," she said.

He did so, and poured himself one, from the decanter on the table between them.

"Where's Jeannie?"

"She is with Mr. Adams," she said, "hopefully fucking his brains out."

"Do you think he was interested in her?"

"Of course," she said. "He's a man, isn't he? He was interested in both of us."

"How was supper?"

"Extremely delicious, as usual," she said, "and very, very interesting."

"Interesting?"

"Mr. Adams is a very interesting man," she said. "Not at all what I expected."

"What did you expect?"

"Well," she said, "I expected something of a, well, barbarian."

"And he was not?'

"Not at all," she said.

"But he can't be a gentleman."

"That depends on what you'd call a gentleman," she said. "Let's just say he had excellent table manners, and leave it at that."

"Well, all right, then," the man said, "but . . . did he agree?"

"He agreed to meet with me tomorrow," she told him, "in private."

"But did he agree to help you?"

"We didn't discuss it in detail, not at the restaurant," she said.

"Why not?"

"Too many ears."

"So then you won't really approach him until tomorrow?" he asked.

"That's right."

"Do you think he'll agree?"

"Oh, he'll agree, all right," she said confidently, sipping her drink.

"How can you be so sure?"

She batted her eyelashes at him and said, "Have you ever known a man to say no to me?"

Clint approached Jeannie, slid his hands around her waist. He found the catch there and released it, then drew the zipper down. The dress came away from her body, exposing her breasts. He was surprised not to find support garments underneath. He thought all the women in Louisiana wore them.

"I don't like corsets," she told him, as if reading his mind. "They make me feel . . . confined."

He pulled the dress off her. There was a wisp of a garment around her hips, and he tugged that down to the floor. She stepped out of it and kicked it away, kept her hands over her head, which lifted her smallish breasts. He cradled them in his hands, the nipples hard against his palms, and squeezed them. She closed her eyes.

Her skin was pale and smooth. He kissed her neck, and her shoulders. The sweet smell of her skin was heady. Abruptly, he lifted her in his arms and carried her to the bed, and she said, "Yes!"

TEN

The mayor of Baton Rouge looked up from his desk as his engineer, Ed Pearson, entered the office.

"Ed," he said, "hey. Have a seat. What can I do for you?"

"Well . . ."

"Come up, speak up, man," the mayor said. "I've got things to do, you know."

"Yes, sir. We, uh, have a problem."

"With what?"

"Well . . . the river."

"We have a problem with the Mississippi River?" the mayor asked.

"Uh, yes, sir," Pearson, said, "that's the river I'm talking about."

"Don't get smart with me, Ed," the mayor said. "What do you mean, we have a problem?"

"Well, it's raining upriver—hard."

"And what's that got to do with us?"

"It's affecting the river."

"In what way?" the mayor asked. "Don't make me drag this out of you, Ed."

"The river is rising—it's rising fast."

"Don't we have levies?"

"We do, but they're not strong enough or high enough to withstand the river at the rate it's rising."

"So what do you suggest?"

"We need to reinforce them."

"Then do it."

"I'll need extra men."

"Hire them."

"Don't you need to check this with the town council?" Pearson asked.

"Do you think the river will wait while we call a meeting of the council?"

"Well, no, sir."

"Then get your men and put them to work," the mayor said. "If Baton Rouge floods, it's not only your job, it's your head. You got that?"

"Yes, sir."

"Then get out—and send in my secretary."

Pearson rose and rushed out of the room. Moments later Mrs. Posey, the mayor's secretary for his two-and-a-half terms in office, came in.

"Sir?"

"I need the members of the town council to meet—today. Send word."

"Yes, sir," she said, "right away."

As she hurried out, he wished that everybody who worked for him would react that quickly when he spoke.

Capucine Devereaux stood up and said to the man across from her, "You have to give me a ride home."

"No problem."

"Now."

"What's the hurry?" he asked.

"I need to check on my girls."

"I thought Jeannie was with Adams."

"She is."

"Isn't she your best girl?"

"She is," she said. "What has that got to do with the others?"

"I don't know," he said, "I'm just saying—"

"Well, don't," she said. "Come along, I need to get back."

"Can I finish my drink?"

"No," she told him. "You don't need any more to drink."

He stared at her, shaking his head, as he got to his feet.

"You think Clint Adams will respond to this bossy attitude of yours?"

"Clint Adams will respond to me the way most men do," she said. "Don't worry."

"Come on," he said. "We'll go out the back. We wouldn't want the respectable members of this club to see you leaving. They might revoke my membership."

As they both moved toward the door, the man suddenly reached out, grabbed Capucine, and backed her into the wall, pressing his body against hers.

"What do you think you're doing?" she demanded.

"You know what I'm doing," he said, leaning his face into her neck.

Abruptly, she reached down, grabbed his testicles through his trousers, and squeezed.

"Jesus, Cappy—" he said, but she squeezed harder and choked off his words.

"If I squeeze just a little bit harder," she told him, "you won't walk straight for days. Now, back up and get off me."

He backed away, his hands held up and out, and she released her hold on his jewels.

She turned and went out the door, assuming he'd be following.

ELEVEN

Jeannie Bartlett was a very talented girl.

The shy woman who had been at supper with Clint and Capucine was gone. In bed, she was inventive and daring.

Her body was supple and flexible beyond any he had ever encountered. At one point he was driving his penis into her, and she had her ankles up behind her head, spreading herself as wide as she could for him.

Another time she was astride him, but with her back to him, riding him, bouncing up and down so energetically he felt like a bronc being ridden.

And her energy never seemed to wane. At one point he woke from a deep sleep, finding her sucking on his hard cock avidly. After exploding into her mouth—she not releasing him from the suction of her lips until he was dry—he checked the time and saw that he'd only been asleep an hour.

"Jesus, don't you get tired?" he asked her, sometime after that.

"I just want to make sure you're nice and happy," she told him.

"I'm happy," he said, "believe me, I'm happy, but I could use some sleep."

"Oh," she said, "well, okay, I could use some sleep myself."

She proceeded to draw the sheet up to her neck, turn her back to him, and fall asleep. He went back to sleep himself, wanting to get as much shut-eye as he could before she woke him again for more.

The sun was streaming in the window when he awoke. Lying next to him, Jeannie was snoring gently. He checked the time and saw that this time he'd been asleep for five hours.

He settled down on his back, stretched, and regarded the ceiling as he replayed the events of the previous evening. Jeannie had barely looked at him, or even spoken, during the entire meal, but once they were away from the restaurant—and away from Capucine—she changed from a shy young lady into a whore—well, practically a whore. No money had exchanged hands, but she did things with him even a whore probably wouldn't have done—although he couldn't be sure, since he did not make use of whores. Even as a young man, he'd been pursued by women of all ages, so he'd had no need of prostitutes.

He turned his head and looked at her. The sheet molded itself to her body, so that he could even make out the crack of her ass. He felt himself stir, and figured this time he'd wake her up.

He pressed himself against her, slid his hand down to her butt, rubbed her through the sheet, ran his finger along that sweet crack.

"Now who doesn't need sleep?" she asked, but she turned into him . . .

Clint watched as Jeannie got dressed to leave. He had offered to buy her breakfast, but she said she had to get back.

"Will I see you later when I meet with Cappy?" he asked.

"No," she said, "I won't be there. She'll want to talk to you alone."

He didn't ask when he could see her again, and was surprised when she didn't ask. Most women did.

She turned to him when she was dressed and smiled. It looked like a very practiced and professional smile.

"Thanks for a great night," she said.

"It was great for me, too."

"Bye."

She went out the door without looking back.

Clint had never paid for a whore, but he had a feeling this was what it felt like when you had.

He had breakfast in the hotel, just to get it over with. Maybe another morning he'd take more time and find a real good place for it. Today, he wanted to eat and get out. When he left, he found Henri waiting out front, seated in his cab.

"Hey," the young man called when he saw him, "good mornin', boss."

"What are you doing out there?" Clint asked.

"Waitin' for you, boss," Henri said. "I figured you'd have someplace to go today."

"Actually, I do," Clint said. "Several places."

"Well," Henri said, "let's get started."

"Okay," Clint said. He climbed into the back of Henri's cab.

"Where to, boss?" the young man asked.

"The sheriff's office."

Henri turned and looked at Clint.

"Really?"

"Really."

"Got a crime to report?"

"Henri," Clint said, "are we going to talk or are you going to drive?"

"I'm drivin'," Henri said.

TWELVE

"Another visit so soon?" Sheriff LeBlanc asked as Clint entered. He was still seated behind his desk as if he had never left it.

"I just have a few more questions to ask you, if you don't mind," Clint said.

"Well," LeBlanc said, waving him to a chair, "have a seat and fire away."

Clint sat and the sheriff folded his arms.

"First, Sheriff," Clint said, "I would like to know why you told Capucine Devereaux that I was in town, and where I was staying."

"Oh, that . . ." The sheriff looked embarrassed. "Well, the fact is I knew she needed help, and that I couldn't offer that help. I simply thought that you—being the man you are—might be able to. I hope you're not too angry with me."

"No, no," Clint said, "I'm not angry. I was just . . . curious."

"Good," LeBlanc said, "I'm glad."

"Now I'd like you to tell me something about the Devereauxes."

"What do you want to know?"

"Whatever you know."

He shrugged and said, "He's very rich, and she's very beautiful."

"Is he older than she is?"

"Oh, yeah," LeBlanc said, "and his family goes way back here in Louisiana."

"And her?"

"She's not from here," the lawman said.

"Where is she from?" Clint asked, even though he already knew.

"Ireland, I think."

"Right from Ireland to here?"

"That I don't know," the sheriff said. Clint didn't know either. "No, I don't think so. He didn't meet her here, but he didn't meet her in Ireland either. I think maybe it was New Orleans."

"Why would she come from New Orleans to here?" Clint asked him.

Sheriff LeBlanc shrugged and said, "I guess because . . . he brought her here."

"And what does she do?"

"Whataya mean, do?" LeBlanc asked.

"Come on, Sheriff," Clint said, "she sent me to my hotel last night with her 'assistant.' This girl knew more about sex than any assistant I ever met. My bet is she's a whore. That would make Mrs. Devereaux a madam."

LeBlanc didn't speak.

"Probably a high-class madam, with her husband's money behind her, eh?"

"Well . . ."

"Don't make me ask her to her face," Clint said. "I'm seeing her again this afternoon."

"Yeah, well, okay, she runs some high-class whores."

"Does she have a house?"

"No," LeBlanc said, "her girls go to her clients' homes and hotel rooms."

"And is her husband a pimp?"

"He's the moneyman," LeBlanc said. "He's just financing her business, but he's not involved."

"You sure?"

"Positive," LeBlanc said. "He's a legitimate businessman."

Clint didn't know how legitimate the man could have been if he was funding a prostitution business, but he let it go.

"What do you plan to do with this information?" the lawman asked.

"Nothing," Clint said. "I just want to know who I'm dealing with. Do you know what her problem is?"

"We never went into it," LeBlanc said.

"It's not somebody trying to take over her business, is it?" Clint asked. "I wouldn't want to get caught between rival prostitution rings."

LeBlanc shrugged and said, "You'll have to find out from her."

"I'll do that," Clint said. He stood up. "Thanks for talking to me."

"Sure."

"One more thing."

"What's that?"

"Don't talk about me to anyone else, understand?" Clint asked. "I don't like it."

He gave the young lawman credit. He bristled, and came back at him.

"Is that a threat?" LeBlanc asked. "I am the law, you know."

"I understand that," Clint said, "and I respect it. I'm just telling you I don't like it when people talk about me. I'd appreciate it if you didn't do it anymore. I don't think that's a threat, do you?"

The lawman calmed down a bit and said, "Well, no, I don't."

"Then we understand each other?"

"We do."

"Have a good day, then," Clint said, and left the office.

THIRTEEN

The stalker rode into Baton Rouge, completely certain that Clint Adams had not yet left. Even if he had, he'd be able to track him down again very easily. His tracking abilities were second to no one. But Adams was here. He'd obviously gotten himself a hotel with the intention of staying awhile. That was okay with the stalker. He could use some time off the trail himself.

Funny. Ever since he'd started trailing Adams, he'd begun to think of himself as The Stalker, and not by his own name. It was his name, and it was what he was doing. He wasn't tracking Adams, or following him, or hunting him, he was "stalking" him, and always from a distance.

This would be the closest he had been to the Gunsmith in weeks. Only he hadn't yet decided if he was going to let Adams see him. That was a decision he'd have to make as soon as he found him.

Capucine Devereaux stepped down from the carriage in front of her pied-à-terre, and then turned to speak to her driver.

"Now you understand what you are to do, right?" she asked.

"Yes, ma'am," he said. "Go to the Cajun House, pick up

Clint Adams, and drive him directly here. No stops along the way."

"Very good," she said. "Go."

"Yes, ma'am."

But he didn't drive off until he saw that his employer had gone into her building safely.

Clint was back at the hotel in plenty of time to be picked up by Cappy's driver.

"Why can't I drive you, boss?" Henri asked. They were standing by his cab.

"I told you, the lady is sending her personal driver for me."

"Is he better than me?"

"I don't know, Henri," Clint said, "but that's not the point."

"How about I follow you?" the young man asked. "In case you want to leave in a hurry?"

Clint was about to say no, but then thought better of it.

"You know," he said then, "that's not a bad idea."

"Yes!"

"But at a distance," Clint said. "I don't want the driver to know he's being followed."

"He won't know a thing," Henri said, "I swear."

"Okay," Clint said. "I'm going to go and wait by the front door. Move your cab so he doesn't see it."

"Yessir!"

Henri pulled his cab away as Clint walked up to the front door. The hotel was small and didn't have its own doorman, so Clint stood there alone, waiting.

A hansom cab pulled to a stop in front of the hotel and a thickset, middle-aged man stepped down and came walking up to the door. Clint had only ever seen hansom cabs in New York.

"Mr. Adams?" he asked.

"That's right."

"My name is Simmons," he said. "I'm Mrs. Devereaux's driver."

"Good to meet you."

The two men shook hands.

"Are you ready, sir?"

"I'm ready."

Simmons nodded and led the way back to his carriage. He waited while Clint climbed aboard, and then got up into his seat.

"We're off, sir!" he called.

"Let's go!"

The carriage started moving, and Clint hoped Simmons wouldn't see Henri following behind.

FOURTEEN

The carriage stopped in front of a small house that was part of a row of small houses with not much space between them. It had two floors, and the second floor had a balcony—or what in Baton Rouge was called a "gallery," which was a balcony supported by posts or columns that reached the ground.

"This is it, sir," Simmons said.

Clint stepped down to the sidewalk and approached the door. Simmons didn't wait for him to go out, just flicked his reins at his horse and drove away.

The door was opened by Capucine herself, wearing a lavender robe that was tied at the waist.

"Clint," she said, "right on time. Please, come inside."

As he stepped past her, she surprised him by kissing him on the cheek, then closed the door behind him.

"Come with me. We can have some lunch in the back, on the patio."

He followed her through the small but well-appointed rooms. He assumed the second floor had the bedrooms. On the first was a sitting room, a small dining room, and an even smaller kitchen.

They passed through all those rooms to an outdoor patio, furnished with wicker chairs and a matching table. The floor was made of flat slate stones. It was the kind of area he didn't see much in the West—but Louisiana was different, especially New Orleans, and now, he supposed, Baton Rouge.

"Have a seat and I will bring you some coffee," she said. "Lunch will be here in minutes."

"Be here?" He had noticed that there was nothing cooking in the kitchen.

"Oh, God," she said, "I hope you didn't think I was cooking? No, no, I don't cook. I'm bringing lunch in from outside." There was a knock at the door just then and she said, "And there it is. I'll be right back."

As she left, he looked up, saw that there was another gallery on the back of the building, overlooking the patio. He wondered if the entire floor, front to back, was a bedroom.

When Capucine came out, she was carrying the coffee. Behind her was a man in a white waiter's jacket, carrying the food.

She put the coffeepot and cups down on the table, and the waiter laid out the food.

"What do we have here?" Clint asked.

"Po' boys, sir."

"What?"

"That's all right," Capucine said, "I'll explain it to Mr. Adams. You can go."

"Yes, ma'am."

The waiter left and Capucine poured the coffee and sat down.

"These are roast beef sandwiches," she said. "The roast beef is almost chopped up, the bread is called a baguette. It has a crisp outside crust, but a soft center."

"Is there gravy?" he asked.

"Lots of it. Try it. You'll like it."

He picked up the sandwich and tried to take a bite without dripping gravy all over himself. It was worth the effort.

"This is delicious."

"I knew you'd like it." She picked hers up and ate it like a sailor. She got gravy all over her chin, but didn't seem to mind.

"I'm glad to see you not trying to eat it like a lady," he said.

"Believe me, you can't eat something like this with lady-like bites."

Clint sipped the coffee and found she had made it good and strong.

"I paid attention last night, when you kept telling the waiter to make the coffee stronger. I hope it's to your liking?" she asked.

"It is," he said. "So was your assistant, by the way."

"Ah, you like Jeannie?"

"I liked the Jeannie who came back to my room with me," he said. "Not so much the Jeannie who was your quiet, mousy little assistant at the restaurant."

"So she came alive for you at your hotel?"

"Alive?" he asked around a bite of sandwich. "She was a regular little whore."

She studied him around her sandwich, then put hers down and stared at him.

"I told her to go easy."

"Easy?" he asked. "She almost killed me."

"So her secret is out."

"Cappy," he said, "I'm afraid your secret is out. I found out some things about you."

"Oh?" she asked. "You mean the sheriff has a great big mouth?"

"I think turnabout is fair play, don't you?" he asked.

"You're probably right," she said. "So, what do you think you know?"

"You're a high-class madam."

"Thank you for the 'high-class.'"

"Does your problem have anything to do with your business?" he asked.

"Does it make a difference?"

"It does," he said.

"Are you a prude, Mr. Adams?"

"I think you only need to talk to Jeannie—is that her real name?"

"It is."

"Well, ask her if I'm a prude."

"Very well," she said. "My problem is not directly connected to my business."

"Not directly?" he asked. "Sounds to me like you're hedging a bit."

"Okay," she said, "let me put it this way. I'm not exactly sure if it's connected to my business or not. That's part of what I want you to find out."

He bit into his sandwich, chewed very deliberately, and didn't say anything.

"Just listen to my sad story," she said. "After that, if you don't want any part of it, I'll understand."

"So I just have to listen?"

"Right."

"And I can finish my sandwich?"

"Yes."

"All right," he said, "start talking."

FIFTEEN

"There's a man," Capucine said.

"Isn't there always?"

"Well, actually there are two men," she added. "The one I'm having trouble with, and the first man I tried to get to help me."

"What was the problem with him?"

"He was more interested in helping himself."

"To what?"

"Well, first my girls, then me, and then my husband's money. Now I can't get rid of him."

"So you want me to do it?"

"If you can dissuade him along the way, that would be great," she said, "but that's not my primary concern."

"Then what is?"

"I'm being stalked."

Join the club, he thought. It was the first time he'd thought about the man following him since the day before.

"By who?"

"I told you," she said, "a man."

"Do you know who he is?"

"No."

"Or what he wants?"

"No."

"How do you know he's stalking you?"

"Because he's always there. Every time I turn around. He doesn't seem to be making a secret of it."

"Do you think it has something to do with your business?" he asked.

"I don't know."

"Or your husband's business?"

"It could."

"Is he being stalked, too?"

"No."

"Have you told him you are?"

"Yes, I have," she said. "He just thinks I'm imagining things."

"What about the second man?" Clint asked. "Does he know about him?"

"Well . . . no."

"Oh, I see," Clint said. "And is he going to know about me?"

"Maybe . . . if I have to tell him."

"Well, if I decide to help, I'll want to talk to him, see what he knows."

"Very well, but I'll be paying you."

"I'll remember that . . . boss."

"So you'll do it?"

"Maybe," he said, "maybe I will if you show me the upstairs."

She turned in her chair and looked up, then looked back around at him.

"You want to see the upstairs?"

"Yes."

"It's just my bedroom."

"I like galleries," he said. "Especially the one in the front."

She stared at him for a few moments, then shrugged and said, "Oh, all right. Come on."

She took him to an outer stairway so that they ended up on the back gallery.

"This do anything for you?" she asked.

"No," he said, "I like the one in the front."

"Okay, come on."

The upstairs turned out to be as he'd suspected, all one room, her bedroom. She led him through it to the front, but before she could open the French doors to the gallery, he said, "Wait."

"You said you wanted to see."

"First I want you to see," he said.

"See what?"

"Tell me if you see your stalker on the street," he said. "If you spot him, let me know where he is. Then I'll step out and have a look."

"Oh, I see," she said. "All right."

She opened the doors.

"Do it casually."

"All right."

She stepped outside, leaned on the railing, looked both ways, then looked up, as if she were just taking the breezes on her face. It felt like rain to Clint, like any minute.

She came back in.

"There's a man there, but it's not him."

"Did you see his face?"

"Well, no, I haven't ever seen his face."

"Then how do you know this isn't him?"

"He has a distinctive build, sort of blocky. Plus when he sees me looking at him, he always steps out into the open."

"Then who is this?"

"Lee Keller," she said. "He's the man I told you I thought might help me."

"And he became a problem."

She nodded.

"So you've got two men stalking you."

"Yes."

"Okay, where is he?"

"Off to the right, across the street, and several doors down."

"All right," Clint said. "Wait here."

He stepped out onto the gallery and looked around. The breeze on his face told him there was definitely rain coming, and probably a lot of it. He looked left first, then up, then looked off to the right where she said the man was. He saw someone standing in a doorway, but he didn't step out, he stayed put. But Clint could see his blocky size.

He turned and went back in.

"Okay, I got him," Clint said. "You wait here."

"What are you going to do?"

"I'm going to try and end it right now," Clint said. "Stay inside, don't go out on the gallery. In fact, stay in this room until I get back."

"Wait," she said. "Do you have a gun?"

"I do," he said, taking the Colt New Line from the back of his belt.

"That little thing?"

"It's not the size of the gun that matters," he said. "But don't worry, if the job goes on from today, I'll start wearing my holster and Colt. Now stay here."

"Yes, sir."

He went downstairs.

SIXTEEN

Clint went down the way he had come, the outside stairway in the back, and then worked his way to the front of the building. He risked a look out onto the street. The neighborhood was quiet and there was no foot traffic to speak of. He could see the doorway in question from where he was, but he didn't know if the man could see him.

He had come around the right side of the building, which had been a mistake. He decided to go back the way he had come, and work his way around to the left side. From there he walked down the street, away from the man in the doorway, then crossed over. On the same side of the street now, he kept as close to the buildings as possible and started making his way toward the doorway. If he could catch the man, he could end the whole business right there and then for Capucine.

He had moved the Colt from the back of his belt to the front. Now, as he approached the doorway, he put his hand on the gun, ready to draw it if the man was armed.

Finally, he was one doorway away and he moved quickly. When he got to the doorway in question, it was empty. The man must have seen him coming.

He looked at Capucine's building and saw her out on the

gallery. That was what had happened. She had come out to
see what was going on, and had tipped the man off by
doing so.

Shaking his head, Clint crossed the street and walked back
to the building.

The man watching Capucine was indeed named Lee Keller.
He made his living with his hands and his gun. He'd heard
that Capucine Devereaux was looking for help, and went to
see her. She had hired him, but by then he was obsessed with
her. He wanted her, and he started hanging around her, making no bones about the fact that he was crazy about her. She
wasn't having it, though, and had finally fired him, because
he had not done the job. His lust for her had robbed him of
his ability to do so.

And he hadn't been able to shake it off. He wasn't working
now; he was just watching her, waiting for his opportunity to
step in and make her his. And he was making no secret of it.
Whenever he could, he let her know he was there.

When he saw her on the gallery the first time, he'd stepped
out of the doorway. Then another man appeared. Was this
someone else she was hiring now? He didn't know the man
on sight, and he ducked back into the doorway so the
man couldn't see him.

But it was easy to see that the man was trying to get a look
at him. When he withdrew from sight, and then Capucine
came back out on the gallery, it wasn't hard to figure out what
the man was planning to do.

Keller decided not to have a showdown with this man until
he knew who he was. So he left the doorway and walked hur-
riedly up the street.

By the time Clint Adams had come out onto the street,
Keller was already gone.

Clint went up the stairs, met Capucine as she came out onto
the back gallery.

"What did I tell you?" he asked.

"I'm sorry," she said. "I wanted to see what was happening. I saw him run up the street, but I didn't want to call out to you."

"It didn't matter," he said. "You'd already tipped him off that something was up. He decided not to wait to find out what."

"Do you think he knows who you are?"

"I hope not," Clint said. "I'd like to keep that our secret for a while."

"So what should we do now?"

"I think we have to be ready to spend a lot of time together."

She pulled at the tie on her robe and said, "I think that can be arranged."

SEVENTEEN

Capucine's body was completely different from Jeannie's. Most notably different were her breasts, which were large, with pendulous undersides, and large, turgid brown nipples. She stripped her robe off, and the filmy garment beneath it, which left her naked. She cupped her breasts in her own hands, popping the nipples with her thumbs.

"I'm not a whore, if that's what you're thinking," she told him. "I just very much enjoy sex."

"So do I," he said, "but I'm not sure this is wise." He was thinking about what Jeannie had said about Cappy getting him into her bed.

"Don't tell me that little whore Jeannie wore you out?" Cappy asked. "You don't strike me as the kind of man who . . . tires easily."

He knew she was trying to play on his ego, but that wasn't the reason he went ahead. He was simply faced with a nude body he could not take his eyes off of. Where was the harm? She may have been married—he didn't usually dally with married women—but it certainly didn't sound like a solid marriage.

As he moved toward her, she dropped her hands. He slid his hands beneath her breasts, feeling their weight and the

smoothness of her skin. Her nipples poked out at him, easily
the longest nipples he'd ever seen on a woman. He lifted her
breasts to his mouth so he could kiss her, lick and suck the
nipples while she sighed and dropped her head back.

Her scent was not as sweet as Jeannie's; it was more subtle
and mature. While he pressed his face to her breasts, she
reached between them for his belt.

"Wait," he said, stepping back.

She gave him a puzzled expression as he looked around.
Eventually, he settled on a place to set his gun where it would
be within easy reach.

"Let's lock these doors," Clint said. They locked both the
front and the back French doors, and then locked themselves
in an embrace, settling into a deep kiss that went on for a long
time. It was so obvious how much Capucine enjoyed kissing.
She was in no hurry to pull back, and allowed her hands to
roam over him as they kissed. Finally, the heat of her body
was what pushed them apart. He had to get out of his clothes,
so they both went to work and quickly stripped him naked.
Then another long embrace, this time with his hard cock
trapped between them.

He slid his hands down her back to her ass, which was
smooth and majestic. He gripped it tightly, pulling her to him,
then skid one finger down the crack, which formed a deep
cleavage that gripped his finger so tight it gave him other
ideas.

She reached between them, gripped his hard cock, and
used it to tug him to the bed. But instead of pushing him down
on the mattress, or lying on it herself, she went to her knees
in front of him, holding his cock in her hand. She licked it,
first the head, then the shaft, wetting it thoroughly before
finally taking it into her mouth.

She sucked him avidly, holding him with her hands on his
butt and bobbing her head back and forth. He started moving
his hips in unison with her movements, and she moaned as
his cock slid in and out of her mouth.

Eventually, he felt he had to pull free of her mouth or it would all be over much too soon. He reached for her, pulled her to her feet, and pushed her down on the bed. Instead of joining her, however, he kept her near the edge of the mattress and knelt down. He tossed her legs over his shoulders, then leaned in and breathed her scent before diving in with his mouth and tongue.

She gasped as his tongue touched her, first entering her, then moving up and down her moist slit, wetting it and finding her hard little clit. He flicked it with his tongue tip and she jerked, as if receiving small electric shocks.

She reached down to hold his head in her hands as he continued to lap at her, Finally, he felt her legs trembling and then she was flopping about on the bed, trying to push his mouth away from her, but he continued to lick and suck at her while she was climaxing, knowing how much more sensitive she was during that time.

"Oh, oh, oh," she cried out, and then instead of trying to push him away, she pushed herself away from him, skittered back on the mattress, and rolled herself up into a ball.

"Jesus," she gasped, "where did you learn to do that?"

"I picked it up over the years," he said, stroking her back.

"God, it was so good . . . it was . . . almost painful," she said. "I didn't want you to stop, but you had to stop." She unfurled her body and looked at him. "Did you learn that from some whore?"

"I've never been with a whore," he said, and then added, "well, I've never paid for one. Let's put it that way."

"If you can do that to a woman," she gasped, "I can see why you wouldn't need a whore. They must line up at your door."

"Maybe," he said, "if I had a door, but I move around a lot."

"No home?" she asked.

"None to speak of."

"Never had a wife?"

"No."

"Ever come close?"

He hesitated, then said, "Once."

"What happened?"

"She died."

"I'm sorry."

Her breathing returned to normal, and she reached out for his cock, which was still semierect.

"Your turn," she said. "Help me turn down the bed so we can do it right."

Together they pulled down the quilt and sheet, then got in the bed together. They cuddled and kissed for a bit, until his cock was standing at full mast, and then she pushed him down on his back and straddled him. First, she rubbed her pussy over his shaft, wetting it with her juices. Finally she lifted her hips, held him with her hand, and settled down on him, taking the length of him into her steamy depths.

"Ahhhh!" he said as her heat engulfed him.

She leaned over, hung her breasts over his face so he could lick and suck them, then leaned down farther to kiss him and say, "Stay with me, Mr. Adams. I like a nice long ride."

He let his hands glide up and down her back and said, "I'll do my best, ma'am."

EIGHTEEN

There were two stalkers in Baton Rouge.

Lee Keller was Capucine Devereaux's stalker. But before he could continue, he needed to identify the man who was apparently spending the afternoon with her. The man who might know that would be her driver, Simmons.

Keller knew where Simmons spent his afternoons when Capucine was at her pied-à-terre. There was a small saloon several blocks away. Simmons would park his carriage out front, and then go inside and nurse two beers for the afternoon.

Keller found the saloon. It was called Casey's. As he entered, he saw Simmons sitting at a table alone, half a mug of beer in front of him. In the past Keller had observed Simmons through the front windows. He usually sat alone, and rarely talked with anyone. So getting into a conversation with him would take some doing. Fortunately, Keller had done his research on the man.

"Simmons" was a British name. Keller knew that Capucine was Irish. There was enough of a similarity there for the two of them to have found each other in the United States.

Keller went to the bar and ordered a beer. The saloon was sparsely populated, and would probably stay that way until early evening. Keller nursed his beer and was able to watch Simmons through the mirror behind the bar.

He waved the bartender over.

"Yes, sir?"

"Can you tell me who that fella over there is?"

The bartender looked.

"I don't know, but he comes in here a lot and sits there alone."

"Always alone?"

"Yup," the bartender said. "Never talks to anyone."

"That's strange," Keller said. "Drinkers usually talk to each other. Do you think he'd talk to me?"

"Beats me. Why would you wanna talk to him?"

"Like I said, drinkers usually talk to each other."

"He only ever drinks beer," the bartender said. "I wouldn't exactly call him a drinker."

"Well," Keller said, "nobody else in here looks worth talking to."

The bartender looked around at the other three or four customers and said, "You've got that right."

"By the way," Keller asked, "do you know who belongs to that carriage outside?"

"Sure," the bartender said, "the fella we're talkin' about."

"What a coincidence," Keller said.

When Clint left Cappy's pied-à-terre, his legs felt weak. The woman was insatiable, and might have convinced him to stay in bed all day, but he needed to get started.

She watched him dress and teased him with her bare breasts before he finally made his escape. She told him she would be there each and every afternoon, in case he wanted to get in touch with her.

"Alone?" he asked. "I mean, I wouldn't want to interrupt anything."

"I will be alone, and very lonely," she said, "until you come back."

"I'll need your husband's address, Cappy," he said.

"What for?"

"I'll need to talk to him about your problem," Clint said.

"But why?"

"I need to convince myself that he's not behind your troubles."

"But why would he—you mean, you think he's having me followed?"

"I won't know until I talk to him," Clint said. "The address?"

She gave it to him.

NINETEEN

Simon Devereaux's office was in a business section of Baton Rouge. Cappy may not have wanted him to talk to her husband because he didn't believe her, but Clint needed to eliminate the man for his own benefit.

When he came out of Cappy's place, he found young Henri waiting there with his carriage.

"Lift, sir?"

"Where have you been?"

"Keeping out of sight, like you said," the young man answered.

"You did a good job of it," Clint said. "I didn't see any sign of you when I came out before."

"I saw the lady's driver head off, so I thought you'd be needing me."

"Good guess." Clint climbed into the carriage.

"Where to?" Henri asked.

Clint gave him the address Cappy had given him for her husband.

After a short drive, they arrived at a three-story building. Clint entered and presented himself to an attractive, middle-aged woman seated behind a desk.

"I'm here to see Mr. Devereaux," he said.

"Do you have an appointment?"

"I don't," Clint said, "but I think he'll see me."

"Why do you think that?" she asked, arching her eyebrows at him.

"Because it's about his wife."

For a moment a look of disapproval crossed the woman's face.

"I'll tell him you're here. What is your name?"

"Clint Adams. Just out of curiosity, what floor is he on?" Clint asked.

She stood and said, "It doesn't matter. Mr. Devereaux owns the whole building. But his office is on the floor above us, so if you'll just wait?"

"Yes, of course."

She disappeared through a door. Clint looked around. The reception area of the building was better furnished than many high-class hotels he'd been in. Simon Devereaux must have had a lot of money.

The woman came back and said, "Will you follow me, please?"

"Yes, thank you."

She took him through that doorway and up a flight of steps to the second floor, then led him to a closed door. She knocked then opened it.

"Mr. Devereaux, this is Clint Adams," she said. "Mr. Adams, Simon Devereaux."

"That's fine, Maddy," Devereaux said. "Thank you."

"Yes, thank you, Maddy," Clint said.

She stared at him then turned and walked away. He watched. She had a nice shape on her, and might not have been as old as he'd originally thought.

"Mr. Adams?" Devereaux said. "Would you have a seat, please?"

"Sure."

Clint closed the door, then walked to the desk. The two men shook hands, and then Clint sat.

Simon Devereaux was in his sixties, a well-kept man, six feet tall and fit. The office was expensively furnished in burgundy and gold.

"You told Maddy this is about my wife?" Devereaux asked. "What has she done now?"

"It's not what she's done, sir," Clint said, "it's what's being done to her."

"Oh," Devereaux said, "is this about that business of her being followed?"

"Yes, sir, it is."

"How did she convince you to work for her on this?" her husband asked. "It's a figment of her imagination."

"With all due respect, sir, I don't think so."

"Why?'

"I've seen the man."

"You've seen the man following her?"

"Watching her."

The man studied him.

"Wait a minute," Devereaux said. "Clint Adams. I know that name."

Clint didn't say anything.

"The Gunsmith, right?" Devereaux was suddenly very animated. "Cappy's got the Gunsmith working for her?"

"I suppose so."

"And you believe she really does have somebody watching her, following her?"

"Yes."

"You've seen him."

"I have."

"And you're going to try to help her?"

"I am."

"And just what is Cappy giving you to do this?" Devereaux asked suspiciously.

"The fact is, I don't like the idea of a man stalking a woman," Clint said. "It's a matter of principle."

"I see."

The man stared at Clint, who simply stared back.

"What do you think I can do to help you?" Simon Devereaux asked.

"Well, you can tell me if you're having your wife followed for any reason."

Devereaux folded his hands on his desktop and studied Clint a bit longer.

"Do you know what my wife does?"

"You mean, for a living?"

"A living?" Devereaux asked. "She doesn't need to do anything for a living. I'm very rich, Mr. Adams."

"I know that, sir."

"What she does, she doesn't do for a living," the man went on. "She does it because she likes it. Damn her, she likes it."

TWENTY

"How do you feel about her running whores, then?" Clint asked, figuring they might as well get it out in the open.

"I detest it."

"Then maybe you'd have somebody watching her."

"And waiting for a chance to do what?" Devereaux asked. "Kill her?"

Clint shrugged.

"Whoever he is," the man said, "he's not working for me. I can assure you of that."

"What about an enemy?"

"Of Cappy's?" He laughed. "One thing about her is she's got no enemies. Everybody likes Capucine—including me, God help me. Did you know I gave her that name? Capucine?"

"No, I didn't know that."

"Do you know what her real name is?"

"I don't know that either," Clint said. "We haven't gotten that close, your wife and me."

"Huh," Devereaux said. "Give it time."

"And what about you?"

"What about me?"

"Enemies?"

"Oh, hell," the man said, "when you're as rich as I am, you've got lots of enemies."

"The kind who would go after your wife?"

"I doubt it."

"Why not?"

"They know I'd have them killed if they did that."

"What if they killed you first?" Clint asked. "Then would they go after her?"

"For what reason?" Devereaux asked. "If I were dead, they'd already have what they wanted."

"Okay, so maybe they plan on killing her first, to make you suffer."

Devereaux thought that over.

"You've got a name in your head right now," Clint said. "You're thinking of the one person in Louisiana who might try that."

"What are you, some kind of mind reader?"

"I don't have to be a mind reader," Clint said. "That's what I'd be thinking right now. Who is it? What's the name?"

Devereaux hesitated, then said, "Jacques Pivot."

"And who is he?"

"My biggest competitor."

"And where does he live?"

"The bayou."

"Not in town?"

"He never comes to town," Devereaux said.

"How does he get things done?"

"He has people who do it for him."

"And how does he contact them?"

"He has a telegraph key at his house."

Clint thought that over. There was no way he could leave Baton Rouge to check that out. Not with a man still stalking Cappy. And not when Keller was still around, the man she thought would be her protector, who was now her other stalker. He wondered then if she and Keller had gotten as far as her bedroom.

"Now what are you thinking?" Devereaux asked.

"I'm weighing my options."

"So you don't think it's me?"

"No."

"Why not?"

"I believe you."

"What if it is me?"

Clint stood up.

"I didn't come here to play games, Mr. Devereaux," he said. "I'm convinced it's not you. Let's just leave it at that."

As Clint walked to the door, Devereaux asked, "Are you going to be asking for my help?"

"I'm not going to ask you for anything."

"No money?"

"I'm not for hire," Clint said. "Your wife knows that, but she asked for my help as a favor. I'm satisfied with that."

He went out and retraced his steps down to the first floor.

The woman looked up from her desk when Clint came out of the office.

"Maddy," he said, "is that short for Madeline?"

"It is."

"Madeline what?"

She hesitated, then said, "Ewing."

"Can I call you Madeline?"

"If you like."

"Madeline," he said, "I get the feeling you don't like Mr. Devereaux's wife."

"Does that matter?"

"Well, Devereaux told me there's nobody who doesn't like her. How do you feel about that?"

"He means men," she said. "There are no men who don't like her."

"And is that why—"

"That's all I'm going to say, Mr. Adams," she said. "I have work to do."

"All right," he said, "I'll respect your wishes. Thanks, anyway. But Mr. Devereaux said you could supply me with an address for a man named Jacques Pivot."

"Yes, of course." She proceeded to look up the address and write it down on a piece of paper for him.

"There," she said, handing it to him.

"Thank you."

She did not look up at him as he left the building

TWENTY-ONE

"Lemme buy you another one," Keller said to Simmons.

"I'm afraid I've already had more than my limit," Simmons said.

"Come on, come on," Keller said, "us drivers got to stick together, don't we?" He slapped Simmons on the back.

"Oh, very well," Simmons said. "One more."

"Attaboy!" Keller said to his new friend. "I'll go get 'em."

He went to the bar and told the bartender to draw two more beers.

"I don't know how you did it," the man said as he set the beers down on the bar, "but you got him talkin'."

"You just have to find somethin' that you have in common," Keller said.

He carried the mugs of beer back to the table and set them down. He wasn't as drunk as he appeared, but neither was Simmons as drunk as Keller thought he'd be by now.

"Thank you, mate," Simmons said.

"So you got to pick your boss up soon," Keller said. "What's he like?"

"He's a she," Simmons said, "A lovely lady with a lot of class."

"Well, lucky you," Keller said. "And I guess she's lucky to have you to protect her."

"Oh, I don't protect her," Simmons said, "I just drive her. Being a bodyguard is not part of my job."

"Oh, I see."

Keller didn't think Simmons was going to say more, but the man drank down half his beer and then started talking.

"She has herself a very special champion at the moment," he said.

"Oh? Who would that be?" Keller asked.

Simmons glanced around and this was the first time Simmons looked even slightly drunk.

"His name is Clint Adams," he said. "Does that ring a bell with you, my friend?"

"Clint Adams," Keller said. "You don't mean . . . the Gunsmith?"

"Exactly," Simmons said. "I thought the man was just a Western legend, but he is actually here, and working for . . . my employer." He wasn't drunk enough to give up her name.

"That's really something," Keller said.

Simmons took a pocket watch from the vest pocket of his suit and said, "Oh, I must go. She needs to be picked up precisely on time."

"Well, you go ahead, my friend," Keller said. "It was good talking to you."

Simmons stood, a bit unsteady, and said, "Thank you for the drinks, sir."

"Don't mention it," Keller said. "It was my pleasure to buy drinks for another driver."

Simmons nodded and walked a bit unsteadily out the door to his carriage.

So, Clint Adams. Capucine had herself a very impressive bodyguard. But Keller wasn't worried. He was more than a match for some Old West legend who was getting long in the tooth.

He sat back in his chair and proceeded to finish his beer in a leisurely fashion.

* * *

There was a driving rain as Clint left the Devereaux building, looking at the piece of paper in his hand. Pivot had an address in a town called New Iberia, in Iberia Parish on the Bayou Teche. It meant nothing to Clint in terms of distance. He was going to have to find out from someone what he was dealing with. How far was Iberia Parish, and what was it like? Would it pay for him to go there?

He could think of only two people to ask—either Sheriff LeBlanc, or Cappy herself. He decided to try the sheriff first.

"Where are we headed, boss?" Henri asked as Clint once again got into the young man's cab. Henri had raised a half roof on the cab to keep the rain off his passenger.

"Sheriff's office."

"Gotcha."

Henri picked up the reins, but at that moment the horse reared.

"What's the matter with him?" Clint asked after Henri got the animal under control.

"He's been that way since the rain," Henri said.

"He doesn't like rain?"

"Not this rain," Henri said. "There's something different about it."

Clint looked up at the sky, put out his hand, and looked at the rain as it landed on his skin. It looked like a normal rain to him.

"Let's go!" he said.

"We're going," Henri assured him. This time when he flicked the reins, the horse simply started forward.

It seemed as if Sheriff LeBlanc never went out on rounds of his town. He was always behind his desk when Clint walked in.

"Well," LeBlanc said, "don't tell me I'm becoming your favorite person in Baton Rouge."

"Hardly," Clint said, "but you are my favorite source for information."

"Well, pour yourself some coffee and take a seat."

Clint poured some coffee, saw that LeBlanc already had a cup, so he just sat down across from the man.

"What's on your mind?"

"Bayou Teche."

"Don't tell me you want to go there," the lawman said.

"I don't want to," Clint said, "but I may have to. How far away is it?"

"Well, it's probably about fifty miles from here to Bayou Teche, but what town do you want to go to?"

"New Iberia."

"Ah," LeBlanc said, "Iberia Parish is more like ninety miles away."

Clint frowned and sipped his coffee. That was not good.

"What do you know about a man named Jacques Pivot?" he asked.

Now it was LeBlanc's turn to frown. "Does this have to do with Mrs. Devereaux's problem?" he asked.

"It might."

"Jacques Pivot is her husband's biggest rival," LeBlanc said. "I would say they're the two richest men in Baton Rouge."

"But Pivot doesn't come to Baton Rouge."

"Still, he conducts his business from a Baton Rouge address, even though he lives in Bayou Teche just outside of New Iberia. Ah, I see. You're thinking of going to see him?"

"Only if I have to."

"He doesn't see many people," LeBlanc said.

"I'll deal with that when the time comes," Clint said. "That is, if I decide to go and try to see him."

"When will you make up your mind?" the lawman asked.

"Not sure," Clint said. He wanted to tell LeBlanc as little as possible about Cappy's business. He put his coffee cup down on the sheriff's desk and stood up. "I still need some more information before I make up my mind."

"Well," LeBlanc said, "come on back if you think I can help further."

"Appreciate that," Clint said, and left.

TWENTY-TWO

Clint decided to find out from Cappy what she knew about Jacques Pivot, but he'd do it the next day. No point in going back to her place so soon. Maybe it would pay to stop in at a local newspaper and read some old issues about both Devereaux and Pivot. It might tell him who was the good guy and who was the bad guy in that relationship.

Clint found his way to the offices of *The Baton Rouge Advocate*, discovered that they also archived old copies of *The New Orleans Times-Picayune*, as well as *The Daily Iberian* from New Iberia.

He settled down in their morgue to leaf through old issues of the newspapers, spent hours going back several years until he thought he had an idea what kind of men Simon Devereaux and Jacques Pivot were.

He left the newspaper after finding a water closet in the building where he could wash the newspaper ink off his hand. He stopped at a small café to have supper alone and think about what he'd learned that day.

Luckily, the café he stopped in was not French and he was able to get himself a good ol' steak and potatoes meal. He washed it down with beer, then had a slice of apple pie and some coffee for dessert.

From the accounts he had read in the newspapers of the business dealings of both Simon Devereaux and Jacques Pivot, he'd discovered that both men were ruthless in their practices. Their selfishness also came across on the page. And then, in the end, their rivalry stood out. At one time or another, each had been known as the wealthiest man in Louisiana. But who held that distinction at the moment he didn't know.

With a full belly, Clint headed back to his hotel.

Keller left the saloon an hour after Simmons had gone. Now that he knew the name of the man working for Capucine Devereaux, it would be easy for him to find out what hotel Clint Adams was staying in. Keller had enough contacts around Baton Rouge to accomplish that without much difficulty.

Once he had the Gunsmith's location, he would show Capucine which man was the most dangerous, which one was most worth her time.

Clint Adams may have been a legend of the Old West, but he was in Baton Rouge now, and in Louisiana, it was Lee Keller who ruled the roost.

The rain came to Baton Rouge.

But it had been raining to the north for days and even weeks. And the excess water fed into the Mississippi, flowing down to the Gulf of Mexico. And the river's levels rose, flooding places like Vicksburg and Natchez.

And now the river was rising in Baton Rouge . . .

The mayor looked over the levee and the river. Standing next to him were the members of the town council, and the engineer, Ed Pearson.

There were men down at the river's edge, working on reinforcing the levee.

"This doesn't look good, Ed."

"Sir," Pearson said, "the river is rising faster than we can build."

"Then get more men, Ed," the mayor said. "The last thing we need is for our city to flood. If that happens, I'm not taking the blame, do you understand?"

"I understand, sir," Pearson said.

"Gentlemen," the mayor said to the others, "let's get back to City Hall."

TWENTY-THREE

By morning the rain had not stopped. In fact, it had increased.
It kept Clint inside, once again having breakfast in the hotel
dining room.

"It's really pouring out there," he said as the waiter brought
his steak and eggs.

"They are saying the city might flood," the waiter said.
"They are working on the levees, but the river is rising too
quickly."

"Has it happened before?"

"Yes, sir," the waiter said. "Both New Orleans and Baton
Rouge have flooded before. It's devastating to the city."

"Well," Clint said, "I suppose the city has men working
on it."

"Yes, sir," the waiter said. "That's what we hope." But the
waiter's tone did not seem very hopeful.

The man walked away and Clint started on his breakfast.

Outside, across the street, standing in the rain, Lee Keller
watched the hotel. He was waiting for Clint Adams to come
out. His intention was to follow the man and wait for his
opportunity.

* * *

Capucine looked out the front window of her house, the house she shared with her husband. The driving rain made it hard to see, but she thought there was a man across the street, watching.

"What is it?" Simon Devereaux asked from behind her. "Do you see someone out there?"

"I'm not sure," she said.

"Well," Devereaux said, "you have a man who is supposed to be taking care of this for you, don't you? Clint Adams?"

"Yes." They had discussed her hiring of the Gunsmith the night before.

"Then let him handle it," Devereaux said. "What about your girls?"

She turned and looked at him.

"What about them?" she asked.

"Anybody following them?"

"Not that they've mentioned."

"So it's only you."

"I suppose."

Devereaux shrugged into his overcoat.

"You're going out in this rain?"

"I have to go to the office," he said. "Why don't you just stay inside?"

"Maybe I will."

"And why not let your girls stay in?"

She folded her arms and said, "They have work to do."

"Well, so have I," Devereaux said. "I will see you to-night."

She just nodded and watched him go out the door.

Across the street the man stood in the rain and watched as Simon Devereaux got into his carriage and instructed his driver to move on.

This left Capucine Devereaux in her house, alone.

But he wasn't ready to take advantage of that.

Not quite yet.

So he remained where he was, the sky raining down on him, watching, and allowing himself to be watched—if she could even see him through the driving rain.

TWENTY-FOUR

Clint found Henri waiting outside, sitting beneath his own half roof.

"Just getting an idea of how the passenger feels," he told Clint. He hopped down, noticed that today Clint was wearing his gun and holster, but he didn't comment on it. "Where are we off to today?"

"We're going to visit a lady at home," Clint said. "Let's get moving and I'll give you the address."

Clint got in and Henri climbed up top.

"Sorry to make you drive in the rain," Clint said.

"It's my job, boss."

Clint gave him the address and Henri flicked the reins. His horse shied, but the driver quickly got him under control, and they were off.

When the cab pulled to a stop in front of the house, the man watching backed into a doorway, out of the rain, out of sight.

Clint stepped down from the cab, asked Henri, "Would you like me to ask the lady to let you wait inside?"

Henri looked at the two-story house, standing on a block

filled with similar, large, blocky shapes in the rain well beyond what his means were or ever would be.

"I'll sit in the back and wait," Henri said. "It'll be dry."

"Suit yourself."

"I always do," Henri said with a smile. In that moment the young man looked no more than eighteen, although Clint figured him to be at least twenty-five.

Clint walked up to the door and knocked.

Cappy opened the door and came into his arms.

"I'm so glad you're here."

"I'm all wet," he said, pushing her away, but not hard. Only at arm's length.

"Come inside," she said, grabbing his arm and pulling.

He entered and closed the door behind him.

"I think he's out there," she said.

"Who? Keller?"

"No," she said, "him. The one."

"Where?"

"Come."

She brought him to the front window.

"Across the street."

He looked out the window. It was hard to see anything in the rain. He could, however, see Henri's cab, with the young man sitting in back.

"Are you going to go out after him?" she asked.

"No," he said. "I'm going to play it differently this time."

"How differently?"

"Let him watch," Clint said. "Come on, I could use some hot coffee."

"Coffee?"

"Yes, coffee. You can make coffee, can't you?"

"I have someone who can make it, yes."

"Well, all right," he said. "let's have some."

Puzzled, she said, "Come with me."

* * *

She left him in the dining room at a long teakwood table and went into what he assumed was the kitchen. She came out alone and said, "Coffee will be here soon."

He shivered a bit.

"You need an overcoat."

"I'll have to buy one if this rain continues."

"Nonsense," she said. "Wait here."

This time she did not go into the kitchen. She went back into the entry hall and then he heard her going upstairs.

An older woman came out of the kitchen, carrying a tray with a pot of coffee and two cups.

"Where is madam?" she asked.

"She'll be back," Clint said. "My name is Clint."

"Sir?"

"Clint Adams."

"Mr. Adams," she said, setting the tray down. "Shall I pour?"

"Please."

She poured a cup for him, and one for Cappy. She executed a small curtsy and returned to the kitchen.

When Cappy reappeared, she was carrying a coat.

"Take this."

"That's your husband's," he said, "and it's expensive."

"Don't worry," she said, setting it down on the chair next to him. "He won't miss it. He has many. And it will keep you—and your gun—dry."

She walked around and sat across from him, added sugar to her coffee.

"What have you been up to?" she asked.

"I talked to your husband."

"How did that go?" she asked. "Did he accuse you of sleeping with me?"

"Not exactly," Clint said. "But I told him that ours is a business relationship."

"Did he believe you?"

"I'm not sure. But he insisted that he hasn't hired anyone to follow you, and I believe him."

"What else have you done?"

"What can you tell me about Jacques Pivot?"

"Pivot?" She laughed. "He is what my husband will become in ten years' time."

"But they're rivals now, right?"

"Jacques may be Simon's rival," she said, "but he is also his idol. Can you understand that?"

"I can."

"What do you think Jacques's part in this is?" she asked him.

"I thought he might be having you followed," Clint said, "maybe waiting for a chance to kidnap you, or worse."

"To get at Simon?"

"Why else?"

She sipped her coffee thoughtfully.

"That thought had never occurred to me."

"And now that I've brought it up?"

"Well," she said, "I always thought Jacques liked me."

"Liked you . . . how?"

"He's rather old," she said, "so I thought, perhaps, like a . . . daughter? Or a niece?"

"So you don't think he'd hurt you?"

"To get at Simon? Or to make a profit? Jacques would sell his mother for that."

"So you do think he could be behind this."

"He could," she said, "but I doubt it."

"Well," he said, "that doesn't help me decide whether or not I should go and see him."

"I doubt that he would see you, unless . . ."

"Unless what?"

"Unless I go with you."

Clint's first instinct was to say no, but then he thought better of it. If he went to the bayou to see Pivot, that would leave

Cappy unprotected. Taking her with him would protect her, and give him a better chance of seeing the man.

"That's a possibility," he said. "When I make up my mind to go and see him, I'll let you know."

"But . . . who else in town would you suspect?" she asked.

"Well, we've talked about your husband's biggest rival," he said. "Who is yours?"

TWENTY-FIVE

Stalkers had come not in pairs, but in threes.

If not for the driving rain and gray weather, the stalkers might have seen one another.

Cappy's stalker was across the street, paying special attention only to her and her house. He didn't even worry about the man who was inside.

Lee Keller was also across the street but at the other end of the block, watching Clint Adams.

But the man who had been stalking the Gunsmith for months, he saw everyone and everything. He found it all very interesting, and amusing. What had Clint Adams found himself involved in?

He could have killed the other two men. It would have been fairly easy to slip up behind them and cut their throats, since they were concentrating only on their prey. But he decided to do what he had been doing for all these months—watch.

He had managed to locate Clint Adams in his hotel by disregarding Baton Rouge's flophouses and palaces. Clint Adams didn't often go slumming, but neither did he try to live high.

This was all very interesting.

*   *   *

"Where are you going now?" Cappy asked as she walked Clint to the door.

"I'm going to see your friend, Monk Rathko."

"Not my friend," she said with a shudder. "He's a horrible man who treats his women horribly. They're always bruised. What man wants to bed a girl who's covered with bruises?"

"I guess his prices are good."

"His prices are cheap, yes," she said, "but so are his girls."

"Then how does he compete with you?"

"Did you hear me say his prices are cheap?" she said. "My God, the man has nickel weekends."

He didn't tell her that nickel whores were nothing new west of the Mississippi.

"You'll have to be careful," she said. "Monk is a monstrous man. He's killed men with his bare hands. And he has—what would you call them?—henchmen."

"Don't they all?"

"How will you find him?"

"I'll probably have to go back to my prime source of information in Baton Rouge."

"Who is that?"

"The sheriff."

"Has he been helpful?"

"He helped you, didn't he?" Clint put his hand on the doorknob. "Keep this locked. Do you have a gun in the house?"

"I do," she said.

"Can you use it?"

"I can, but do you think I'll need to?"

"It seems to me your man is pretty content right now just to watch." He knew what that was like. His own stalker had spent months doing just that.

When Clint got out to Henri's cab, the young driver climbed onto his perch. Clint got in and was glad for the borrowed coat. Cappy had been right—it was keeping him and his gun dry, well, drier.

"Hey, boss, there's a fella across the street watching the house."

"I saw him."

"Both of 'em?"

"Both?"

"One behind us, one ahead of us," Henri said. "But I think the one behind is watchin' the house, and the one ahead of us is watchin' you."

"You've got good eyes."

"I spend most of my time on the street, boss," he said. "I gotta have good eyes."

That gave Clint a thought.

"Hey, Henri, what do you know about Monk Rathko?" he asked.

"I know enough to stay away from him," Henri said. "He gets a piece of every crooked nickel in town."

"Do you know where to find him?"

"Why would you want to find him?"

"I'd like to talk to him."

"You'd have to go down by the river," he said, "and right now there's the danger of a flood."

"Maybe we can get in and out before that happens."

Henri turned in his seat.

"You sure about this?"

"Positive."

"What about these two fellas?"

"Well, if you're right, one of them will come with us," Clint said. "I think the other one will stay right where he is for a while."

"Gonna get pretty wet."

"I don't think he could get much wetter."

TWENTY-SIX

The engineer, Ed Pearson, had more men working on reinforcing the levee, but the rising water was still ahead of them. Most of them were ankle deep in the Mississippi waters. Pearson watched from a higher point, directing them as best he could. He knew his job depended on fighting back the big river, but it seemed to be a losing battle.

Henri drove Clint right to the edge of the docks, but stayed away from the river's edge.

"There's a saloon about a hundred yards in," he told Clint. "It's called Blood 'n' Guts."

Clint had been to many dock saloons with the word "Blood" in the name.

He climbed down from the cab.

"You got a problem with waiting here?" he asked the younger man.

"I'm good," Henri said. "They're used to seein' me down here."

"Okay," Clint said, "wait here as long as you can."

"Sure, boss," Henri said, "but watch your back."

"I usually do."

Clint left Henri there and walked onto the docks. He wondered if Cappy's stalker, Keller, was watching.

Keller had managed to hear what Clint and Henri were saying, and knew they were heading for the docks. He wasn't able to follow, but even in the driving rain he was able to find himself a cab eventually and had it take him to the docks.

When he got there, he saw Clint Adams's cab sitting there, waiting, so he knew he wasn't far behind.

He had his cab let him off down the street, paid the fare, and then made his way to the docks.

Cappy sat at her dining room table with the gun set down in front of her. She had never used a gun, but she thought she would be able to if it was in self-defense. She hoped it wouldn't come to that.

She hoped Clint would be back . . . soon.

Clint approached the Blood 'n' Guts Saloon without a plan. He decided when he reached the door that the best thing to do was just walk right in and ask for Monk and not show himself to be a threat to the man.

The problem with this kind of saloon was that everybody knew everybody, and a stranger walking in attracted a lot of attention—sometimes unwanted attention.

As he stood in front of the door, he looked down and was surprised to see running water at his feet. Not a torrent, but enough to tell him that the levee certainly was not holding. Better to get his business here done and get away from the river.

He opened the door and went in.

Keller found Clint just before he went into the Blood 'n' Guts Saloon. Keller knew what kind of place it was, and he himself usually avoided it. He knew Monk Rathko was not a man to be trifled with.

He decided to wait outside.

As Clint entered the crowded saloon, it fell silent and every-one turned to look at him.

"A man could drown out there," he said, breaking the silence.

TWENTY-SEVEN

The man stalking Clint didn't follow him to the docks; he followed Lee Keller. He wasn't sure what Keller's intentions were when it came to Clint, and if the man had bad intentions toward the Gunsmith, he wanted to be there to stop him.

He did not want anyone else killing Clint Adams . . .

Clint walked to the bar and asked, "Can I get a beer, please?"

The bartender didn't answer, but he drew the beer and put it in front of Clint—then he glared at him because Clint was dropping water on the bar.

"Oh, hey, I'm sorry," Clint said. He took a step back and wiped at his face and hair with both hands, but it didn't help much.

"Here," somebody said, "try this."

He turned and saw a huge man tossing him a less than clean towel. It had already been used, but it would do the trick to get himself somewhat dry.

"Thanks." He dried his hair, face, and hands with it, then tossed it back.

"The beer's on the house, Dan," the man said to the bartender.

"Yes, sir."

The man was monstrously huge, with a big black beard and a wild head of black hair. His sleeves were pushed up so that the black hair covering his forearms was very evident. Given the bartender's reaction, he assumed this was Monk Rathko.

"Thanks," Clint said.

"Seems to me you might prefer coffee, though," the man said. "At least it would warm you up."

Clint sipped the beer and then said. "You might have a point."

"Why don't you come with me and we'll have some?" the man suggested.

Clint studied the big man for a few seconds, sipped the beer again, and then asked, "What have I done to deserve this kind of treatment?"

"Well," the man said, "it ain't every day we get somebody like the Gunsmith in our place. The least we can do is show you some hospitality." He put out a hand the size of a ham. "Monk Rathko."

TWENTY-EIGHT

Clint shook the man's hand, mindful of the fact that Monk could have crushed his gun hand very easily.

"How do you know me?" he asked.

"Come on," Monk said, "we'll have that coffee and I'll tell you."

Clint put the beer down on the bar and followed Monk through the saloon. There wasn't an empty chair in the place, and they all watched him go.

Monk took him to a door in the back, and through into an office. There was a potbelly stove there with a pot of coffee on it.

Monk walked to the pot, poured two cups, and handed Clint one.

"Have a seat, Mr. Adams."

Clint was surprised by Monk's civility. Cappy had made him sound like a monster.

The big man sat behind his desk, dwarfing it as he did so. Clint sat across from him.

"How did you recognize me?" Clint asked.

"I have eyes all over the city," Monk said. "They've seen you with Capucine Devereaux."

"And recognized me?"

"No, but they found out who you were and told me," Monk said. "So I've been expecting you."

"Expecting me?"

Monk nodded.

"In fact, I knew the moment you pulled up in your cab. Your driver's out there getting soaked. Would you want to bring him in?"

"I don't think he'd want to," Clint said. "He told me he avoids this place."

"Probably a smart thing."

"Okay," Clint said, "so you know who I am. Do you know why I'm here?"

"I can guess," Monk said. "Capucine's having some trouble and she thinks I'm behind it."

"She doesn't think so," Clint said. "I asked her who her competitor was."

"She has lots of competitors."

"I asked who her biggest competitor was."

"Well," Monk said, "I'm flattered. She has a high-class product."

"She does," Clint said, "but she says your prices undercut her."

"That's true," Monk said. "But my girls can't compare to hers."

"So you don't see yourselves as competitors, at all?" Clint asked.

"I don't," Monk said. "I think our customers are totally different."

The two men regarded each other across the desk for a few moments, sipping their coffee. Clint was surprised that the man's coffee was comparable to the best he'd had on the trail.

"So what's this problem she's having?" Monk asked.

"Somebody's following her," Clint said, "stalking her."

"What do they want?"

"We don't know," Clint said.

"No contact?"

"Not yet," Clint said. "He's just following her, and letting her know she's being followed."

"Sounds like a war of nerves," Monk said. "That's not really my style."

"What is your style?"

"I think you can tell by looking at me," Monk said. "I don't attack somebody's nerves, I break their bones."

"I get it."

"What were you thinking, coming here?"

"Well," Clint said, "to tell you the truth, I was thinking about this. That we'd just talk."

"And why would you believe me when I say I have nothing to do with it?"

"I pride myself on knowing when a man's lying to me," Clint said. "I don't think you have any reason to lie."

Suddenly, Monk turned his head and looked behind him.

"Sonofabitch!"

"What is it?"

Monk leaped out of his chair and rushed to the back door. Clint stood up to look. There was water coming in from beneath the door.

At that point the door to the saloon opened and the bartender said, "Hey, boss, we got water coming in the front door."

"Yeah, yeah," Monk said, "the back, too. It's that goddamned levee." He looked at his bartender. "Get the bags."

"Bags?" Clint asked.

"Sandbags," Monk said. "We've got to block the doors and windows."

"The windows?" Clint asked.

"If the levee goes, it could get that high," Monk said.

"Jesus," Clint said. "Can I help?"

"We'll take all the hands we can get!" Monk said. "Come on."

TWENTY-NINE

Clint worked with Monk, the bartender, and a bunch of the customers to try to fortify the saloon against the oncoming flood.

"What happens if this doesn't hold?" he asked Monk as they piled sandbags in front of the door.

"We'll have to get out of here," Monk said.

"Have you dealt with this before?" Clint asked.

"A few times, but we've never had to abandon the place," Monk said.

They stood back from the door and looked down. So far the water had been stopped.

Clint had a thought.

"What happens out in the bayou when there's flooding like this?" he asked.

"That depends on different levees and whether they hold," Monk said. "Where are you talking about?"

"I might have to go out to Iberia Parish."

"That's Bayou Teche," Monk said. "If the West Atchafalaya Levee goes, it'll pretty much flood the whole area. But there usually has to be a hurricane for that."

"And what's causing this flooding?"

"Heavy rains north of here," Monk said. "Apparently, other

levees are holding, and the water is rushing down to us. If some of the northern levees break, it would bleed off some of the water, and save us."

"Why don't they send somebody upriver to break those levees?"

"Because doing that would flood other towns, like Vicksburg or Natchez, if they haven't already been flooded. Smaller towns than that would be totally wiped out."

"Well, do you think this will hold?"

"No way to tell," Monk said. "The engineers are working on the levee. We'll have to wait and see. If I was you, though, I'd get away from these docks."

"I intend to," Clint said.

"And if the levee fails completely . . ." Monk said.

"Get out of Baton Rouge?"

"No," Monk said, "get out of Louisiana."

Keller looked down at the water running over his feet, and decided to withdraw from the docks. If the levee went, he'd be hip deep in water, or worse.

He headed for slightly higher ground, but if the levee failed completely, he knew he'd have to leave the city. Maybe he should make sure he took Capucine with him.

Simon Devereaux looked out his office window at the falling rain. If he'd been on the town council, he'd know what was going on with the levee, but the mayor and his cronies had made sure that didn't happen. If the city flooded, he was safe where he was, and they had some supplies, but he wouldn't be able to stay in his office for an unlimited amount of time. And if he didn't get out before then, it would take a boat to get out.

He walked to his office door and looked at his assistant, Maddie, seated at her desk.

"Maddie, you better go home," he said. "Fortify your house."

"I live on the second floor," she reminded him.

"Maybe you should just leave town," he said, "before the levee fails."

"What about you, sir?"

"I'm going to go home, get Mrs. Devereaux, and leave."

"Do you think she'll go with you?" I'd go with you, the woman thought. She was hopelessly in love with her boss.

"I don't know," he said. "If she doesn't, I'll just go."

"I could wait—" she started.

He stepped forward and put his hand on her shoulder.

"No," he said, "go now. I don't want to have to worry about you."

"Yes, sir."

She gathered her belongings and left the building. From a window, Devereaux watched her go.

When Clint came walking up to Henri's cab, the young man got out of the back.

"You made it," he said.

"I did."

"Did you see Monk?"

"Yes."

"How did that go?"

"I helped him sandbag his place."

Henri looked down at the water running at his feet.

"I was hoping that was just rainwater," he said.

"It isn't," Clint said.

THIRTY

It was raining even harder, making it more difficult to see, but Clint thought that Cappy's stalker was still in place. He'd lost track of his own, the man Henri had seen. He'd just have to keep watching his back.

"Want me to wait?" Henri asked.

"Yes," Clint said, "and come inside. I don't want you to drown out here."

The door was opened just moments after Clint knocked. Cappy looked confused when she saw Henri.

"This is my driver," he said, stepping in. "We both need towels."

"Of course."

She rushed away and came back with two white towels.

"Come have some coffee and tell me what's been going on," she said.

They followed her into the dining room. Clint saw her gun on the table.

"Have a seat," she told them. "I'll have Mrs. McGovern bring coffee."

"This is some house," Henri said while drying his hair.

"Feeling uncomfortable?"

"Very."

Cappy came back and Clint said, "Capucine, this is Henri. He's been helping me."

"Ma'am," Henri said.

"Hello."

She sat with them. Mrs. McGovern came out with coffee and pie—apple.

"I thought you might need something," she said to them.

"Thank you, Mrs. McGovern."

"Yeah, thanks," Henri said.

The middle-aged cook went back into the kitchen.

While Clint told Cappy about his talk with Monk, Henri shoveled the pie into his mouth.

"So Mr. Monk is out," Cappy said.

"As far as I'm concerned."

"What does that leave us?" she asked.

"Not what," he said. "Who?"

"Jacques."

He nodded.

"So we're going to Bayou Teche?"

"Looks like it."

"In this rain?" Henri asked.

"Maybe there'll be less flooding there," Cappy said.

"Not if the Atchafalaya Levee goes," Henri pointed out. "If that happens—"

"I know," Clint said. "Monk told me." He looked at Cappy. "Pivot has a telegraph key, right?"

"He does."

"Can we get a message to him?"

"No," she said. "The telegraph office wouldn't be open in this weather."

"Then we have to go."

"When?"

"In the morning."

"What about tonight?"

"What about it?"

"That man is still out there," she said. "I'd like you to stay here."

"What would your husband say?"

"He's gone."

"Where?"

"Away from the water, he said," she answered.

"Did he ask you to go with him?"

"He did, but we both knew I wouldn't."

Clint looked at Henri.

"Hey, I'll come back and get you, boss," he said. "Drive you all the way, if you want."

"Can we do it in one day?" Clint asked.

"If it was dry and we drove at night, sure. But now we'll probably have to stop in Lafayette first," Henri said.

"Okay," Clint said, "let's figure on that."

Henri finished his pie and coffee, and Clint walked him to the door.

"Want me to check out that guy who's watching you, boss?" the young man asked.

"I don't want you to do anything but drive, Henri," Clint said.

"But I could—"

"Just drive," Clint said, putting his hand on the young man's shoulder. "Okay?"

"Sure, boss. See you in the morning."

Clint closed the door behind him, and returned to the dining room.

"Does Mrs. McGovern live in?" Cappy asked.

"She does."

"Tell her to stay away from the doors and windows," Clint said. "Maybe she should just go to bed early."

"I'll tell her."

"Is our friend still across the street?"

"Yes."

"You speak to Mrs. McGovern," he said. "I'm going out the back."

"Why?"

"Maybe I can save us a ride to Bayou Teche."

THIRTY-ONE

While Capucine went to tell her cook to go to bed, Clint put on the borrowed coat and went out the back kitchen door. This time, he wanted to try to get to the man before he was seen. He told Cappy in no uncertain terms to stay away from the windows.

It was still raining hard, but he did not allow that to deter him. The rain would help him sneak up on the man in the doorway.

Or so he thought.

When he got to the doorway, the man was gone. It reminded him of his experiences with his own stalker, whom he was never able to sneak up on, or even get a good look at.

These stalkers were very good at their game . . .

When he reentered the house by the back door, he removed the wet coat and set it aside. Cappy came into the kitchen.

"Did you see him?"

"Did you go near the window?"

"No," she said. "You told me not to. This time I listened."

"He was gone," Clint said. "Maybe he was just too wet to stay out there."

"Speaking of which . . ." she said, handing him a towel.

"Thanks."

"I prepared the guest room for you," she said. "I don't want Mrs. McGovern to see us together."

"Good idea."

"Come on," she said, "I'll show you where it is."

She took him upstairs and down the hall to a doorway.

"This is your room," she said. "Mine's at the end. Mrs. McGovern's is at the far end."

"How many bedrooms are there up here?"

"Seven."

"That's a lot of bedrooms."

"Simon sometimes has several overnight guests at a time for business."

"I see."

"What time will we be leaving in the morning?"

"Early," Clint said. "I told Henri to come by at six."

"All right." She kissed his cheek. "I'll see you later."

He thought he knew what that meant . . .

Cappy's stalker was waterlogged by the time he got home. But he was so intent on her that he hadn't really noticed the impending flood conditions of Baton Rouge. He dried himself off and got into bed. He'd get an early start come morning.

Keller had made a new decision.

Clint Adams was in the house with Cappy, where he couldn't get at him. So he decided to follow Cappy's stalker when he left. He was sure the man hadn't seen him. He was focused only on Capucine, which Keller could well understand. Maybe he'd be able to do something to help her, after all.

As for Clint's own private stalker, when he was sure Clint was in for the night, he went back to his own hotel for a good night's sleep. He wasn't sure what he was going to do about the flooding. He might have to leave the city, head for higher ground, and keep watch with his binoculars to see which way Clint Adams went when he left.

Morning would probably tell the tale . . .

Clint lay in bed listening to the rain beat against the windows and on the roof. There seemed to be no end to it. He had no idea what they would find when they got to the bayou. He'd been out there before during visits to New Orleans, but never under these conditions. He had heard talk of past floods, of the dead bodies of animals and people floating in the water. The dead were not buried in the ground in Louisiana; they were interred in crypts. If the water got high enough, it swept the bodies right out of their resting places.

Would this be as bad? He had no way of knowing.

He heard the floor in the hall creak, reached out to let his hand hover over his gun, which was hanging nearby on the bedpost.

The door opened and Capucine slipped in, wearing a nightgown.

"Shove over," she said. "I want you to warm me."

She wanted more than that.

So did he.

THIRTY-TWO

The sex was intense, just this side of violent, and yet quiet so as not to wake the cook, Mrs. McGovern.

They lay side by side later, sweat cooling on their naked bodies.

"I've got one of my own, you know," Clint said.

"Your own what?"

"Stalker."

"Someone is stalking the Gunsmith?"

"Seems like it."

"Why?"

"I don't know," he said. "I haven't been able to get close enough to ask him."

"Why not?"

"Because he's very good at what he does," Clint said, "much like your guy."

"So what's that mean?" she asked. "You're not going to be able to catch him?"

"No," he said, "I'm going to catch your guy. It's my guy I'm going to have trouble with."

"Why do you say that?"

"Because I'll have help catching your guy," he said. "Mine, I'll have to catch on my own—and he's very good at hiding."

"Well," she said, snuggling up to him, "you don't have to worry about it tonight, do you?"

"No," he said, opening his arms for her, "not tonight."

The back door opened slowly and a man stepped in quietly. Mindful, but unconcerned, about the fact that he was leaving wet footprints, he made his way through the house to the staircase. He crept up the steps as silently as he could, avoiding the third step, the one that creaked. He then moved down the hall stealthily and stopped at the door to the room he knew to be Clint's. Only two other doors were closed, the cook's room and Cappy's. That pointed to this room as belonging to the Gunsmith.

He pressed his ear to the door and listened . . .

Clint slipped the nightgown over Cappy's head, baring her smooth but bountiful body. A man who appreciated beautiful breasts, he gave hers all his attention for several minutes. She sprawled on her back while he worked on her, moaning as his mouth moved over both gorgeous orbs. At the same time, he slid his hand down between her thighs. She spread her legs to allow him to press his palm to her hairy bush. She was hot, and already wet. He slid his middle finger up and down her moist slit, and when he touched her "hot button"—as he had heard one woman refer to it—her legs stiffened and she gasped, closed her thighs tightly, trapping his hand there.

His mouth moved from one nipple to the other as he placed his hand on one thigh and pushed her legs apart again.

"You've got to let me in," he whispered.

"I know," she said. "I'm sorry. It was just a reflex. Nobody's ever made me feel the way you do before."

He touched her again, this time with his thumb, while he slid his index finger inside her.

"Oh God . . ." she breathed.

He began moving both fingers at one time, while simultaneously sucking her nipples. The combination was too much for her to bear, and she spasmed, crying out before she could stop herself . . .

The man in the hall heard Capucine cry out. He looked up and down the hall, but the cook did not seem to have heard it.

He pressed his ear to the door, a puddle forming at his feet as water dripped from his shoes, coat, and chin.

He also had an erection . . .

"Jesus," Cappy said as Clint continued his ministrations, "you're going to kill me."

"Do you want me to stop?" he asked with his lips to her neck.

"Are you insane?"

He smiled, kissed her breasts again, then kissed his way down to the apex of her thighs. Before long, his mouth had replaced his hand. As he avidly licked and sucked her, she spasmed again and again . . .

The sounds of Capucine's pleasure excited the man in the hall. He knew the cook's room was down the hall, but she didn't interest him. He had two choices. Burst into the room, or leave.

He turned and made his way back down the hall, downstairs, and out the back door.

Cappy was recovering when Clint said, "Shh."

"I can't say anything anyway," she said wearily.

He got off the bed, grabbed his gun, and padded naked to the door.

"Wha—" she started, but he cut her off with a wave of his hand.

He put his hand on the doorknob, turned it slowly, then yanked the door open. The hall was empty, but when he looked down, he saw the puddle at his feet.

"What is it?" she asked.   .

"Somebody was out here," he said. "Stay inside and lock the door."

She started to say something, but he pulled the door closed as he stepped into the hall, still naked. He followed wet footprints to the stairway, and down. They led him to the kitchen door.

Whoever the man was, he had come and gone.

THIRTY-THREE

While Clint was gone, Cappy caught her breath, stood up, donned her robe, and walked to the window. She looked out, saw the rain-drenched street in front of the house. At first she didn't see anything, but then she thought she saw him. A figure in the rain, in the dark, staring up at her window.

At her.

Clint came back up the stairs, his feet wet from having stepped in the water the intruder had left behind. If he'd learned anything, it was that this man was a watcher, not a doer. He could have slammed the door open and fired on Clint and Cappy while they were in bed. Instead, he chose to turn around and leave.

As Clint passed the cook's door, it opened and Mrs. McGovern looked out. Her eyes widened when she saw him, naked in the hall, but she did not back away, or close her door. In fact, she looked him up and down quite appreciatively.

"Is there a problem?" she asked.

"There was an intruder, Mrs. McGovern," he said. "He's gone now, but please lock your door in any case."

"I will," she asked. "Would you . . . like to come in?"

"Maybe another time," he said.

She laughed, withdrew, and closed the door.

Clint walked back to Cappy's door, tried it, and found it locked.

"Cappy," he said, knocking. "It's me."

She unlocked the door immediately and pulled him inside.

"I saw him."

"Where?"

"Out front."

"You went to the window?"

"Yes."

Clint walked to the window, brushed aside the curtain, and looked out. He squinted, but could not make anything out in the rain.

He turned and saw her looking at him, her arms folded, hugging herself.

"Where was he?" she asked.

"In the house, outside the door."

"While we were . . ."

"Yes."

"My God!" she said. "He could have killed us."

"He didn't even try," Clint said. "All he did was listen."

"What does this mean?"

"Nothing that changes what we're going to do," he said. "We're still going to the bayou, so I suggested we get some sleep."

She looked down.

"Your feet are wet," she said. "Sit down."

He sat on the bed. She fetched a towel and dried his feet. His penis hardened while she did it, but oddly she didn't seem to notice.

"This really has you spooked, doesn't it, Cappy?" he asked.

"Yes."

"Come on," he said. "I'll stay with you all night, but we have to sleep. Right?"

She looked at him and said, "Right."

They got into bed, under the covers, snuggled in close with her head on his shoulder, and before long they had drifted off to sleep.

THIRTY-FOUR

In the morning Cappy packed a small bag. It was on the floor by the front door when Henri arrived with his cab.

"Still raining," he said when Clint let him in, "but it seems to have let up some."

"Okay," Clint said. "Take the lady's bag to the carriage. We'll be right out."

"Yes, boss." Henri picked up the bag, then looked at Clint. "I didn't see anybody out there watching the house. Did you do something last night?"

"No," Clint said, "I guess he just got tired of being wet."

Henri nodded and left.

Clint looked up, saw Cappy coming down the stairs.

"Do you think it's safe for Mrs. McGruder to stay here?" she asked him.

"I think so," Clint said. "Nobody's after her. Our leaving will probably make her safe."

"I'll tell her we're going," she said, and went to the kitchen.

Henri may not have seen anyone watching the house, but they were there. Cappy's stalker was down the street in a different doorway, keeping an eye on the front door. He saw the cab pull up, the driver go inside, and then come out with a bag.

The bitch was going someplace.

Keller saw the same thing, but he was behind the stalker. He decided it was time to act, so that he'd be able to watch Cappy and Clint Adams without having to worry about anyone else.

He eased up behind the man, reached around to cup his chin in one hand and pull it up. The man grunted in surprise, but Keller used the knife in his other hand to cut the man's throat. He let the man slump to the ground, half in and half out of the doorway, and withdrew to see what happened next.

Clint and Cappy came out together and walked to the cab. As he was helping her into the backseat, he looked down the block and saw something. Henri was right—the rain had let up slightly, was no longer an unyielding curtain of gray.

"Wait here," he told Cappy.

"Where are you going?"

"Just wait."

He walked down the block and soon realized he was looking at a body. He hurried across the street to the doorway. The man was lying half in, half out, the blood from his cut throat mixing with the water on the ground. Clint bent down and checked the man's pockets, but came up empty. He stared at the man, saw that he had the blocky build Cappy had described.

He hurried back to the cab, climbed in with Cappy.

"What is it?"

"Somebody killed your stalker," he said. "Probably Keller. Slit his throat and left him in the street."

"Then it's over?"

"Far from over," Clint said. "We've still got Keller to contend with, and whoever sent the dead man will probably just send another—or maybe even more than one."

"Jacques?"

"That's what we're going to find out."

Henri came down from his seat and stuck his head in the back.

"We ready to go, boss?"

"Ready, Henri."

"Uh, where are we goin', boss?"

"Iberia Parish, in Bayou Teche," Clint said.

"Yeah, I know that . . . but where?"

Clint looked at Cappy.

"Don't look at me," she said.

"Have you been there before?"

"One time, with my husband."

"So you remember where it is."

She hesitated, then said, "Not exactly."

"Cappy—"

She looked at Henri.

"Take us to New Iberia, Henri," she said. "Someone—anyone—there will know where to find Jacques Pivot's house. I'm sure of it."

Clint looked at Henri and said, "You heard the lady. New Iberia."

THIRTY-FIVE

It was raining too hard to tell if they were being followed. The roads were waterlogged, but that was from the rain, not from flooding—not yet anyway.

Once, it appeared that one of the rear wheels was stuck in the mud. Both Clint and Henri had to get out and push the carriage while Cappy held the reins. At another time the horse stopped—just stopped. He refused to move for fifteen minutes, then started again. Henri took credit for cajoling the animal, but Clint believed the horse had just decided on his own to start moving.

As they arrived in Lexington, the rain started to come down even harder. There was an inn there, where they were able to secure two rooms.

"One for the lady," Clint lied, "and one for my driver and me."

"Excellent, sir," the innkeeper said.

The innkeeper had someone take care of the carriage and horse. Clint had left Eclipse back in Baton Rouge, having first checked on him before they left.

"Do you need someone to carry your bag, sir?" the innkeeper asked.

"No, no, that's fine," Clint said. "We can handle it fine."

"Very well, sir."

"How full are you on a crazy night like this?" Clint asked.

"Not very full," the man said. "Only one other room is taken."

"Someone else traveling in this weather?" Clint asked.

"Yes, sir," the man said. "I was surprised, too. He arrived just before you."

Before? Clint thought.

"Can we get something to eat?" Clint asked.

"I'll have my wife prepare it," the innkeeper said. "Come down when you're ready."

"Okay," he said to Henri and Cappy, "let's go on up to our rooms."

The three of them went up the stairs. As they walked past the other doors to their own, he wondered which room was occupied.

Since the place was empty, they had managed to get rooms next to each other.

"You're in there, Henri," Clint said.

"But I thought you said—"

"Henri."

"Oh," the driver said, then, "Oh! I see."

"Get settled and meet us downstairs."

"Right."

Clint opened the door to the other room, let Cappy in first, then carried her bag in, closing the door behind them.

"What's wrong?" she asked.

"What makes you think there's something wrong?" he asked.

"I saw your face downstairs," she said. "Is it the other man?"

"Yes," Clint said. "He got here ahead of us. I don't like that."

"Maybe," she said, "he's just an innocent bystander."

"And maybe not," Clint said.

"So how do we find out?"

"I'm thinking," Clint said, "that we should just ask him."

THIRTY-SIX

They met Henri downstairs and they were led into a dining room by the innkeeper, whose name was Cooper.

"Have a seat, folks," Cooper said. "My missus will be right out."

They sat at the long, rough-hewn oak table.

"What about the other guest?" Clint asked. "Isn't he going to eat?"

"He said he'd be down," Cooper said. "I expect him any minute."

"Good," Clint said, "I'd like to see who else is crazy enough to be out in weather like this."

Cooper laughed. At that moment his pretty blond wife came in carrying steaming plates. Her husband introduced her as Milly, and Clint introduced himself and his companions. Mrs. Cooper was about twenty-five, probably half the age of her husband.

"Where's our other guest?" she asked her husband. "Mr. . . ."

"Smith," Cooper said. "He said he'd be coming down."

"Maybe you should go and tell him that the food is ready," she said. "And then help me in the kitchen with the rest of the food."

"I can do that," Clint said. "I can go and get him. Just tell me what room he's in."

"Why, that's right nice of you," Cooper said. "He's in room five."

They were in rooms nine and ten.

Clint stood up.

"I'll go get him and be right back."

He left the dining room and went back up the stairs, then walked to room five and knocked.

"Mr. Smith, the food is ready," Clint said. "Our hosts would like you to come down."

No answer.

He knocked again.

"Mr. Smith?"

Nothing.

He tried the doorknob and found the door unlocked. He opened it and went in.

There was a man lying on the bed.

"Smith?"

He walked to the bed. The man looked like he was asleep, except for the bullet wound in his chest. Clint checked his pulse, found none. He was very dead.

Clint wet through his pockets, then saw his saddlebags hanging on the back of a chair. He walked over and went through them both. In the second one he found a letter addressed to Lee Keller.

If Keller had killed the other stalker, who had killed Keller? And how had Keller known where they were going, so he could get there ahead of them?

Clint looked around for a weapon, a gun or a knife, and found none. He put Keller's letter in his pocket, and withdrew from the room.

He walked down the hall, started down the stairs, and then stopped. There were five people in the house that he knew of, and he knew that three of them hadn't killed Keller.

That left the innkeeper and the innkeeper's wife.

He went down the stairs slowly, his hand on the butt of his gun, even though he knew he probably wouldn't get the chance to use it.

As he entered the dining room, he saw that Milly Cooper was holding a gun on Cappy, while her husband was holding a gun on Clint as he entered the room.

"I know who you are, Mr. Adams, and I know what you can do with a gun. You can probably draw and kill me before I could shoot you. But then my wife would kill the lady."

"I get it."

"I'm going to come over and take your gun from your holster. Please don't try anything."

"I won't."

Cooper approached Clint, who could see that the man's hand was shaking. On the other hand, his wife's hand was rock solid.

The man took his gun from his holster and scampered back, tucking it into his belt.

"Now what?" Clint asked

"Now you do what you were going to do," the man said. "Eat. My wife is a very good cook. Sit."

Clint sat at the table, wondering if Cappy had put her gun in her bag. She was sitting directly across from him.

"Dig in," Milly Cooper said.

"What about you two?" Clint asked.

"Oh, we ate while we were waiting for you to get here," Cooper said.

Clint looked at Cappy and Henri.

"We might as well eat."

"I am hungry," Cappy admitted.

"Me, too," Henri said.

"Let's eat."

There were hunks of beef and pieces of chicken, along with large chunks of potatoes.

"So tell me, Mr. Cooper," Clint said, "which one of you killed Mr. Keller upstairs?"

"Keller?" Cappy asked around a piece of chicken. "Dead?"

"Shot."

"That was me," Cooper said. "It was necessary, once he brought word that you were coming this way."

"So you and he work for the same man?"

"That's right."

"It must have been quite a shock when you shot him dead."

"You should have seen his face."

"And what happens after we've eaten?"

"You go to your rooms," Cooper said, "and you stay there."

"Until when?"

"Until morning," Milly Cooper said. "But first your lady, here, will help me clean up."

"Clean up?" Cappy asked, looking appalled.

"Sure," Milly said. "After all, it is women's work, isn't it?"

THIRTY-SEVEN

There was still more Clint needed to know, but the food was very good, and he was very hungry. So he waited until they were finished eating to ask.

"Come with me, Mrs. Devereaux," Milly said. "We'll get the coffee."

Cappy stood up and started to walk toward the kitchen slowly.

"Oh, no wait," Milly said. "We can't go to the kitchen without some plates."

"Plates?"

"Let's clear the table, ma'am," Milly said.

With a pained look, Cappy started collecting dirty plates and stacking them.

"That's good," Milly said. "You'd make a good waitress."

"And you're very pretty," Cappy said. "You could come work for me."

"I'm afraid I'm not a dirty whore, Mrs. Devereaux," Milly said. "Come along."

Milly and Cappy went into the kitchen, leaving Clint and Henri with Cooper.

"What's next?" Clint asked.

"You folks will go to your rooms and get some sleep . . . or whatever you do."

"And in the morning?"

"We'll have breakfast," Cooper said, "and then go from there."

"Go where?" Henri asked.

"I'll let you know tomorrow. Let's go upstairs."

"I thought we were waiting for coffee," Clint said.

"Right you are," Cooper said. "We'll take you up after that."

Milly and Cappy returned with the coffee, and they sat and drank it while Cooper and his wife watched. While they were watching, husband and wife got together to have a conversation. They spoke low so that they couldn't be overheard, but at one point they began to argue.

". . . not the way it's supposed to be," Cooper said to her.

"Keep your voice down!" she hissed.

"Don't tell me . . ." he started, then stopped and lowered his voice. They continued on with their voices lowered.

"All right," Cooper said finally, "that's enough coffee. Let's go. Time for bed."

They slid their chairs back and stood up. Cappy looked at Milly, as if waiting for her to give her some orders, but the younger woman didn't say anything.

"Up," Cooper said.

Under Cooper's gun they went up the stairs. First they stopped by Henri's door.

"Which of you is in here?" Cooper asked.

"That's Henri," Clint said.

"Inside," Cooper said to Henri, gesturing with the gun.

Henri looked at Clint, who nodded. The young man stepped inside and Cooper closed the door, locking it with a key.

"All right, I assume you two are sharin' a room?" he asked.

"That's right," Clint said.

"Then get on inside and get on with it," Cooper said with a grin.

Cappy went into the room. Clint started in, then stopped and turned to Cooper.

"What do you want?" he asked.

"I want you to get in your room."

"Is this place really yours?"

"Sure it is. Why?"

"I just thought maybe Pivot sent you here to wait for us."

Cooper hesitated, then said, "Who?"

"Jacq—"

"Get inside!"

Clint backed away, and Cooper slammed the door and locked it.

Clint turned and saw Capucine sitting on the edge of the bed.

"What's going on?"

"I'm figuring they work for Pivot," Clint said. "Anybody wanting to go to Pivot's house has to pass through here first. It makes sense."

"And Keller?" she asked. "Why kill him if they work for the same man?"

"That I don't know," Clint said. "Somehow Keller figured out where we were going and got here first. He probably killed the man across from your house, and that man probably worked for Pivot. Maybe he wasn't working for Pivot. Maybe he just got in the way."

"These people are going to kill us," she said.

"No, they're not."

"How can you be sure?"

"Well, for one thing," he said, "I'm not going to let them."

THIRTY-EIGHT

"What about the other thing?" Cappy asked.

"Your stalker never tried to kill you," he said. "I don't think that's what's going on here."

"So then what are they going to do? This man and his crazy bitch wife?"

"Maybe," Clint said, "they'll take us to Jacques Pivot."

"But that's what we want."

"Yes."

"You think they'll give us what we want?"

"If it's also what they want."

She shook her head.

"Now I'm confused."

Clint walked to the window. The rain was still coming down. He tried the window, found it locked. When he tried to open it, he couldn't budge it. Somehow, it had been secured. He could have broken the window, but could Cappy have dropped down to the first floor? And what about Henri? They couldn't leave him behind.

"Are you thinking about going out the window?" she asked him.

"I was," he said, turning away from it, "but I've decided against it."

"Because of me?"

"It's just not a good idea."

"So what do we do?" she asked.

"We go to sleep," he said.

"Sleep?" she asked. "How can I sleep with those crazy people running around with guns?"

"They're not running around," he said. "One of them is probably on guard, and then other is asleep. And then they'll switch."

"So we should wait until she's on guard and make a move," she said.

"Why?"

"Because she'll be weaker."

"Are you sure you just don't want a try at her because she made you clear the table?"

"That, too," Cappy said. "That crazy bitch made me make coffee."

"And it was terrible."

"What do you expect?" she asked. "I've never made coffee before."

"I'll take the first watch," Milly said to her husband, coming up into the hall.

"That's all right," Cooper said. "I'll stay on watch all night."

"Don't be an ass," she told him. "At your age, you need your sleep."

"You're always throwing my age in my face," he said. "You didn't seem to care how old I was when I took you off the streets of New Orleans."

"That's because I didn't know you were going to take me here, to this dump."

"Wouldn't that lady laugh if she found out you really were a whore when I found you?"

"Just go to sleep, Coop," she said. She'd started calling him "Coop" when they met and continued it after they got married.

"I see the way you're lookin' at that kid, Milly," Cooper said. "Like a bitch in heat."

"I don't have any interest in that kid, Coop," she said. "You're imagining it. Now tell me who's in what room and go get some sleep!"

"Bitch!" he said, but he answered her, then went downstairs, where their bedroom was.

Milly turned and looked at the two locked doors. Wouldn't her husband be surprised to find out which of the males she was really interested in?

She reached into her jeans pocket for the key.

"So what do you say?" Cappy asked.

He'd been giving the matter a lot of thought, and she was impatient.

"We'd have to find out which one of them is out there first."

"Why don't we just do what you said before, Clint?" she suggested.

"What's that?"

She shrugged.

"Let's just ask."

"We'd have to knock and see who answers," he said. "If it's him, you'll have to talk to him. If it's her, I'll have to do the talking."

"And then—"

But before they could implement their plan, they heard a key in the lock.

It looked like they were going to find out who was on guard sooner than they thought.

THIRTY-NINE

The door opened and they saw Milly standing in the hall. She pointed her gun at them.

"Come on out, Adams," she said.

"What for?"

"We need to talk."

"About what?" Cappy asked.

"That's none of your business, bitch," Milly snapped at her.

"Who are you calling a bi—"

"Hold on," Clint said. "If she wants to talk, maybe I should hear what she has to say."

"But Clint—"

He placated Cappy with a hand gesture and said to Milly, "Okay, I'll come along."

Milly backed away from the door and said, "Close and lock the door behind you."

Clint did as she asked, pulling the door closed and turning the key.

"Remove the key from the lock."

He did.

"Now come with me."

She backed her way down the hall, keeping the gun on him.

"Where's your husband?" he asked.

"He went downstairs to go to bed," she said. "He won't be back up here for four hours."

"What are we going to do that will take four hours?" he asked.

"You'll see." She stopped in front of a room, kept the gun on him, and opened it. "Inside."

He stepped inside. She kept her distance, or he would have tried to take the gun from her.

It was another bedroom.

"Put the key on the bed," she said, closing the door.

He did as she asked, tossed the key on the bed.

"Grab that chair and put it in the middle of the room."

He grabbed the wooden chair, centered it, and sat down.

"Now wha—" he started as she moved around him, but before he could finish, everything went black . . .

His head was pounding when he woke. He tried to reach up to touch it, but found that his hands were securely tied behind him, and his legs were tied to the chair legs. He also noticed that he was completely naked.

"Welcome back," Milly said.

She was standing in front of him with no gun in her hand.

"What's going on, Milly?" he demanded. "Why am I tied up?"

"Because I need to have my hands free," she said. "I can't do what I'm going to do with a gun in my hand."

"And what is it you have to do?" he asked.

"I'm thirty years old," she said.

"You look younger."

"Thank you," she said. "My husband is over sixty. He's an old man."

"He looks pretty good for over sixty."

"That's not the point," she said. "He can't give me what I want." She walked up to him and stared down at his crotch. "You can."

"Oh, Milly," he said, getting her meaning, "not under these conditions."

"You don't think so?" she asked.

"No."

"I know so."

She reached down and stroked his flaccid penis. Immediately, it jerked and began to swell. She took it in her hand and began to stroke it. It continued to harden, and she smiled.

"See?"

"Milly," he said, "I'd be of much more use to you if my hands and feet were free."

She released his cock and said, "We'll see." She got down on her knees, put her hands on his thighs, and rubbed them. Then she ran her hands up over his chest. "You don't know how wonderful it is to touch a man who is fit."

He was trying to think of something else, but then her hands were on his genitals again. With her left hand, she cupped his testicles. With her right hand, she stroked his cock again. Soon his erection was standing straight up.

"My, my," she said, gazing at it. Her eyes took on a glassy look.

"Milly—" he said, but she wasn't listening. In fact, he was sure she wouldn't hear a word he was saying.

She stood up and backed away, but only long enough to divest herself of her clothes. When she was naked, she put her hands on her hips and posed for him. She had a slender body with good, peach-sized breasts and smooth skin. There was a tangle of fair hair between her legs, and he could already smell her scent. His cock got even harder, damn it!

"Don't worry," she said "I won't hurt you."

FORTY

Cappy was nervous.

She didn't know what was happening to Clint, didn't know when he'd be back—or if he'd be back. She walked to the window and looked out at the rain. For a moment she thought she saw the stalker, but no. Clint said he was dead. Then she thought she saw someone—a figure, not blocky, but tall and slender.

She stared, but the figure would not come into focus for her—and then it was gone.

She turned away from the window, hugged herself, and bit her lip.

"Your woman," Milly said, touching her breasts, "she's not as young as me. Not as firm and smooth."

He didn't answer. His mouth was dry as she teased her own nipples with her thumbs. She then squeezed her breasts in her hands, and moaned.

"Milly, look—" he started, but his voice caught in his throat. The woman standing before him was completely wanton, and she had his attention.

"Don't worry, Clint," she said. "I won't keep you waiting long. I won't keep me waiting long."

She got to her knees in front of him and began to pepper

his naked thighs with hot kisses. He tried to concentrate on something else, but then her mouth was on him, and suddenly he was into it. She was hot and wet and she sucked him avidly, her head bobbing up and down in his lap. He stared down at the top of her blond head and damned his own body for having a mind of its own.

She sucked and sucked him until he was hard as a rock, then she stood and straddled him.

"Now," she said. "I haven't had a hard one in me in a long time."

She reached down for him, held him in place, and lowered herself, just enough to tease her pussy lips with the head of his cock. She kissed his mouth lightly as she rubbed him along her hot slit, and then she lowered herself down and took him inside.

"*Yesssss!*" she hissed, sitting down firmly on him, taking him to the hilt.

"Mill—" he started, but she silenced him with another kiss. Despite the circumstances, she tasted sweet to him. She kissed him hotly, wetly, for a long time, then began to move up and down on him.

"Milly," he said from between gritted teeth, "if you untie my hands, I'd be a lot more active—"

She continued to bounce up and down on him, her arms on his shoulders, her breasts pressed to his face. He tried to resist, but as her nipples brushed his mouth, he reached for one with his tongue and teeth. For a moment he thought of biting down on it—hard—but decided against it. It might make her mad enough to shoot him. Or if she screamed, her husband might come running in, shooting.

As she continued to bounce on his cock, he tried to match her thrusts with his hips, but trussed up the way he was, it was difficult. The smell of her, the taste, the feel, and his inability to throw himself into the activity were all combining to make him very frustrated.

She started to grunt as she came down on him, and he could feel the wet slime of her on his thighs.

"Milly, damn it!" he snapped.

Suddenly, she sat down on him and her eyes came into sharp focus. She was breathing hard, and perspiring. The smell of her sweat and sex was heady stuff.

"What is it?" she demanded.

"Cut me loose so I can move," he said. "It'll be better. I promise."

She leaned back, lacing her fingers behind her neck, and cocked her head.

"You tryin' to fool this little Cajun gal, *cher?*" she asked.

"I didn't know you were Cajun."

"Well, I am."

"I'm not trying to fool you, Milly," he said. "I want to use my hands on you. I want to be with you on that bed." He nodded toward the bed.

She studied him for a few moments, then leaned forward and kissed him. He pushed his tongue into her mouth, gave the kiss all he could.

"You give me your word you won't try anythin' funny, *cher?*" she asked.

"I do," he said. "I give you my word that when you untie me, I won't make a move for your gun. We'll go right to that bed and do this properly."

She closed her eyes and wriggled in his lap. He felt her insides close over him, around him, like a fist.

"All right," she said, "I'm gonna take you at your word."

She got up off him, letting him out of her cunt slowly. She moved around behind him and untied his hands, then crouched in front of him and untied his legs.

Immediately he reached out and scooped her up in his arms. His legs were slightly unsteady from being tied to the chair, but he managed to carry her to the bed.

"Whoa!" she said, but he ignored her. He dropped her on the bed on her back and climbed on with her, covering her with his body.

"Now we're going to do this the right away," he told her.

FORTY-ONE

Clint worked out his frustration—and his aggression—on the pretty Cajun wife. He used his mouth and tongue to give her as much pleasure as she could stand, then drove his cock into her and fucked her for his own pleasure. They both kept it as quiet as they could, not wanting to alert anyone else in the house as to what was going on. In the end he left her lying on the bed, exhausted, sated . . . and careless.

He got off the bed, walked over to where she had left the gun, and picked it up. Then he picked up his pants and slipped them on. He was putting on his shirt when she rolled over in the bed and looked at him.

"Hey—"

"Quiet."

"You said you wouldn't try anythin' funny!" she hissed at him.

"I said I wouldn't make a move for your gun, and we'd go right to that bed. That's what we did." He waved the gun at her. "This is different."

She settled back onto the bed, watching as he pulled his boots on. When he was dressed, he stood up and looked at her.

"Well, now the boot is on the other foot," he told her. "You're naked, and I'm dressed."

She spread her legs so he could see her moist, pink slit.

"What are you gonna do to me?"

"The same thing you did to me," he said. "Come on over to the chair."

"You can't tie me to the chair," she told him. "Cooper will be lookin' for me."

"That's okay," he said, "because I'm going to be looking for him."

"Will you kill him?" she asked anxiously.

"Do you want me to?"

"Very much."

"Come over to the chair."

She got off the bed and walked, jelly-legged, to the chair. He tied her hands behind her, and her legs to the legs of the chair.

"Why do you want your husband dead?"

"Because I want to get away from here," she said. "I'm sick and tired of living with him."

"Help me, then," he said as he finished. She was now secured to the chair.

"Help you how?"

"I want to know who you and your husband work for," Clint said. "And if Keller worked for the same man."

"I don't know who Cooper works for," she said. "I just do what he tells me to do."

"Are you telling me the truth?"

"I am."

"And Keller?"

"Who?"

"The man you killed."

"Oh, him," she said. "No, he didn't work with Cooper. Not that I know of."

"Then why did you shoot him?"

"Coop told me to."

"Again, the truth?"

"No man has ever done to me what you did to me in that

bed, *cher*," she said. "I'm telling you the truth because I hope you'll do it again."

"And if you're a good girl," he said, "I might just do that."

"I'll be good," she said.

"Promise?"

"Promise."

He leaned forward and kissed her on the right nipple, which made her shiver.

"Good."

She smiled at him.

"What do you want me to do first?"

"Tell me where to find your husband."

"That's easy," she said. "He'll be in bed now, on the first floor. I'll tell you where the room is."

"Okay."

"But I want something."

"What?"

"Don't leave me tied to this chair, *cher*."

"I can't let you loose."

"I don't mean that," she said. "Leave me tied up, but put me on the bed."

"Do you want to get dressed, too?"

"Oh no, *cher*," she said. "I don't."

"Why not?"

"Well," she said, "just in case Coop kills you, I want him to come in here and find me just like this—naked, with your sweat and juices on me, and in me."

"You really hate him, don't you?"

"Oh, yes."

"Why?"

"He didn't give me what he promised me," she said.

"All right," he said, "let's get you over on the bed."

Once she was secured to the bed—he'd also wrapped the rope around the legs of the bed—he slipped out of the room and down the hall to the door of the room Henri was in. He had the key to Cappy's door, but not to Henri's. So he put his shoulder to it and forced the door open quietly—or as quietly as he could force a door.

"Clint!"

"Quiet. Come on, Henri, I'm putting you in Cappy's room with her."

"What are you gonna do?"

"Find the owner and see what I can find out."

"Where's his wife?"

"She's tied up. Come on."

They moved down the hall to Cappy's door. Clint used the key and opened it.

"Inside," he told Henri.

"Wha—Clint!" Cappy said. "Where have you been?"

"Never mind."

"You've got a gun?"

"Got it from Mrs. Cooper."

"And where is she?"

"Tied up," Henri said.

"The two of you stay here. I'm going to have a talk with Cooper."

"Are you going to kill him?" she asked.

"Only if I have to."

FORTY-TWO

Clint went down the stairs as quietly as he could, then moved across the first floor according to Milly's directions. He found himself at a closed door. He tried the doorknob, found that the door was unlocked. He opened it slowly, hoping the hinges wouldn't squeak. They didn't.

He stepped into the room, listened, and heard the even breathing of a sleeping man. He waited for his eyes to adjust to the darkness in the room. When he could make out the man in the bed, he moved to it, pressed the gun to the sleeping man's forehead. The man woke up immediately.

"Move and I'll blow your brains out, Cooper," he said.

The man stayed still.

"Where's my wife?"

"Upstairs," Clint said. "She's all right." He saw the man's gun on the night table next to the bed. He grabbed it and tucked it into his belt.

"Light the lamp," he told Cooper. "We're going to have a talk."

"About what?"

"Light it," Clint said. "We'll get to that."

He allowed Cooper to sit up nervously and light the lamp by the bed.

"Now what?" Cooper asked.

"Now you tell me who you work for."

"If I do that," he said, "I'm dead."

"If you don't tell me, I'll kill you right now," Clint told him. "Your choice."

Cooper began to sweat.

"Can I take a minute—"

"No," Clint said. "Answer the question." Clint cocked the hammer on the gun.

"Okay, okay," Cooper said. "I work for Jacques Pivot."

"Doing what?"

"Intercepting people he doesn't want to see," Cooper said. "Anyone coming from Baton Rouge has to go by here first. Like Keller."

"Yes."

"And us."

"Yes."

"How did he know we were coming?"

"That I don't know," Cooper said. "I was sent a message to stop you."

"By name?"

Cooper nodded. "And description."

"How did you get the message?"

"He sent his man."

"Who?"

"A man named Lebeau."

"How many more men does he have with him at his house?" Clint asked.

"I don't know."

"Guess."

"Maybe half a dozen."

"And a wife?"

"No."

"Any women?"

"He's an old man."

"So as far as he's concerned," Clint said, "you've stopped us."

"Yes."

"Because you've stopped every other person he's ever told you to."

"Yes."

"Will he send his man to find out for sure?"

"Yes."

"When?"

"Probably this morning."

"All right," Clint said. "Come on."

"Where?"

"I'm going to reunite you with your wife," Clint said, "but first, tell me how to get to Pivot's house."

FORTY-THREE

When Cooper walked into the room and saw Milly tied up on the bed, naked, his eyes bugged out.

"What the hell—"

"Hello, *cher*," she said. "Did he tell you he had his way with me? It was glorious!"

"What? You—" Cooper turned to Clint, who pointed the gun at him.

"Just stand easy," he said. "Untie her."

Cooper obeyed, and Milly rubbed her wrists where the ropes had chafed her.

"Now you, Milly, tie him to the chair."

"Whatever you say, Clint."

Naked, she started to tie her husband's hands behind him as he sat in the chair.

"Goddamn it, woman," Cooper snapped, "cover yourself."

She stood up, put her hands on her hips, and smiled at the old man.

"Clint likes to see me this way, don't you, *cher?*" She turned to Clint.

"Stop fooling around and tie his feet."

"Yes, lover."

Hearing his wife call Clint "lover" incensed the man, but there was nothing he could do about it.

She tied his feet securely, then stood up.

"There!" she said.

"Now get dressed," Clint said.

"What? But I thought . . ." She looked pointedly at the bed.

"Not now, Milly," he said, "and certainly not in front of your husband."

Pouting, she started to gather her clothes.

Clint walked to the door and called out for Cappy and Henri to come down the hall.

As Cappy and the cab driver came into the room, Capucine saw Milly half dressed, her breasts still naked.

"You bitch!" she said. She took her gun from her bag and shot Milly through the chest, right between her perfect little breasts.

"No!" Cooper shouted from his position tied to the chair.

Cappy turned and shot him in the chest, as well.

"What the hell are you doing?" Clint demanded.

"They're killers!" she said, her eyes wild.

Clint walked to her and grabbed the gun from her hand.

"You had this all the time?"

"Well . . . yes."

"Why didn't you use it before?"

"I was . . . afraid."

"So now that she's half naked and he's tied up, you got brave?"

"I'm sorry," she said, lowering her eyes. "I just . . . lost control."

Clint checked the two bodies. Milly's eyes were wide with surprise, but she was dead. So was Cooper, slumped in the chair with the ropes holding him up.

Henri was standing off to the right, looking very frightened.

"Kid," Clint said, "I still need you, but if you want to turn around and go back—"

"No, no," Henri said, "I'm your man, Clint."

"Okay. We're going on to Jacques Pivot's place. But first, I've got to find my gun."

Clint went back downstairs and searched Cooper's bedroom. He found his gun in the top drawer of a chest. He slid it into his holster, tossed the other guns onto the bed. He went to the sitting room, where Cappy and Henri were waiting for him.

"I checked outside, boss," Henri said. "There's a lot of water. That levee mighta gone."

"We better get going, then," Clint said. He looked at Cappy. "I should leave you here."

"No," she said, "not with . . . them. Besides, you'll need me."

"Why?"

"Jacques is an old man, but he's always had a yen for me," she said. "That's how we'll get in to see him."

"If he has a yen for you, why would he put you in danger?" Clint asked.

"He's a businessman," she said. "If it was good for business, he'd put his own mother in danger."

Clint looked at Henri, who shrugged.

"All right," Clint said. "You got any other weapons on you?"

"No."

He put his hand out for her bag, which was a simple drawstring type. It was light, but he checked inside anyway. No derringers or knives. He handed it back.

"All right, Henri," he said. "I've got directions to Pivot's house. Let's see if we can make it before we're knee deep in water."

FORTY-FOUR

Henri was right about the water. It was ankle deep as they walked to the cab. The horse didn't like it either, but Henri kept him calm.

It wasn't dawn yet, but with the driving rain, it probably wouldn't have looked much different if it had been. The days had been gray, and would probably continue to be so for a while.

The road was all mud and the horse had to work hard to pull the carriage. Then, at one point, they either changed direction or hit higher ground, because suddenly there was less water.

"Is the water receding?" Clint shouted to Henri.

"No," Henri said, "we're movin' further away from the river. If the levee goes, though, it'll catch up to us."

Cappy gripped Clint's arm tightly with both hands.

It took several hours, but they finally came within sight of a large, two-story house with pillars all along the front. The house must have cost a fortune to build—but why would someone build such a house all the way out here?

He posed his question out loud and Cappy said, "Jacques is Cajun. He was born in the bayou, and he loves it."

"Well," Clint said, "I suppose there's something to be said for loving your home."

They drove up to the front of the house. It could have been the gray rain, or the moss clinging to the walls, but up close the house looked to have fallen on hard times.

Henri stopped the carriage directly in front of the door. Clint stepped down and looked around. He was surprised that they had not attracted any attention.

He turned and helped Cappy down. Henri stayed right where he was.

"Do you want to come in?" Clint asked him.

"I think I'll be safer right here," Henri said. "Wetter, but safer."

"I don't blame you," Clint said. "We'll be back soon—I hope."

Clint and Cappy approached the front steps and walked up. Clint might have thought the house was deserted, but for the light in a couple of windows.

They reached the front door and Clint knocked. He was about to knock again when suddenly he heard a lock click, and the door opened.

"Capucine," an old gent said. "What a surprise—and in this weather? Come in, come in, my dear, and introduce me to your friend."

Several people had referred to Jacques Pivot as an old man. If this man was, indeed, Pivot, they were understating the point. This man was so old his skin seemed like translucent parchment paper. There was a map of blue lines beneath his skin, where they weren't obscured by wrinkles.

He closed the door and turned to face Capucine.

"Hello, Jacques," she said. "Allow me to introduce my friend, Clint Adams."

"Ah, the infamous Gunsmith," the man said. "How wonderful to have someone of your import in my house. Excuse me if I don't shake hands, but my bones are very brittle these days. A handshake could actually break my hand."

"I understand," Clint said.

But the old gent's hands weren't too flimsy to lift one of Capucine's to his mouth so he could kiss it.

"Come with me," he said. "We'll get you some coffee—or brandy—to warm you up."

They followed him into a large, opulently furnished living room. He walked to a pull rope against the wall and yanked on it. In seconds a man who looked even older than Pivot appeared.

"Ah, Charles, my guests need to warm up." He looked at them.

"Hot tea for me," Capucine said.

"Of course. And you, sir?"

"Coffee."

"Please," Pivot said, "the brandy. Allow me the pleasure of watching you drink it, as I can't imbibe myself."

"All right," Clint said, and to Charles, "Brandy."

"Yes, sir," Charles said.

"Please, sit," Pivot said.

The chairs were overstuffed, and dusty. Capucine gingerly lowered herself onto the sofa, while Clint chose one of the armchairs.

"What brings you here in such horrible weather, my dear?" he asked.

"Well . . . I'll let Clint explain it, Jacques."

"Sir?" Pivot said, looking at Clint.

Clint was having his doubts, except for the fact that Cooper confessed to working for Pivot.

"Well . . . Capucine had been having a problem with someone stalking her, following her everywhere, and asked me to see what I could do about it."

"And how does this bring you to me?"

"We thought the man behind it might be someone who was, uh, in business with her husband. I've been told you are his closest competitor."

"And why would this lead to having her followed?" he asked.

Clint was surprised the man had not taken a seat, and had chosen to remain standing.

"Perhaps in an attempt to distract her husband from his business practices?" Clint asked.

"Nonsense," Pivot said, waving a skeletal hand. He didn't offer anything further.

"Why is that, sir?" Clint asked.

"I don't have any need to distract Simon Devereaux. I have outfoxed him at every turn whenever we have done business. And I prefer to have him at his best when I do beat him—such as his best may be."

"Sir, do you know a man named Cooper?"

"I do," he said. "He and his wife run an inn in Lexington."

"Do they work for you?"

"Certainly not," Pivot said. "Why would I need an inn? Ah, here are the drinks."

Charles carried a tray to Capucine, who claimed her tea, and then Clint, who took his brandy. He then tucked the silver tray beneath his arm and left. He walked painfully slow, and they waited for him to leave the room before continuing.

"Mr. Pivot, Cooper told me he works for you."

"Doing what? Running the inn?"

"And keeping people away from your house."

"How?"

"Pretty much by killing them," Clint said. "Do you know a man named Keller?"

"Never heard of him."

"And you didn't send anyone to follow Capucine?"

"I did not," Pivot said. "I do not, however, know how to prove that to you."

Clint studied the man, then said, "You don't have to. I believe you."

"Then we drove all the way out here, and went through all of those things at the inn, for nothing?" Capucine complained.

"No, not for nothing," Clint said. "Now we know Mr. Pivot, here, is innocent."

"I am a little too old to be considered innocent," Pivot said, "but I appreciate the sentiment."

"So now what?" she asked.

"I guess we should get back to Baton Rouge," Clint said.

"I wouldn't do that," Pivot said.

"Why's that?"

"I have my own telegraph key in the house," the man said. "Just a short while ago I received a message that the city is under water."

Clint immediately thought of Eclipse, who he had left behind in Baton Rouge.

"The whole city?" he asked.

"Well, a good part of it," Pivot said. "You are both welcome to stay here—at least overnight."

"I was given to understand you don't like guests," Clint said.

"Indeed, I do not," the man said, "but rarely have I had a guest of your stature. And, of course, Capucine is always welcome."

"I have a driver outside."

A pained look passed over Pivot's face, but he said, "He may stay, as well."

"Well," Clint said, "I don't think we have much of a choice."

"I will have Charles show you to your rooms. You will, of course, have dinner with me."

"Thank you, Jacques," Cappy said.

"Yes," Clint said, "thank you."

Pivot pulled the rope again. As slowly as Charles moved, he was right there. Clint didn't know how he did that.

FORTY-FIVE

Charles showed Clint, Capucine, and Henri each to their own room.

"We have bath facilities," he told them.

"I would like a hot bath," Capucine said.

"Yes, ma'am."

Clint and Henri both declined the offer, but they had pitchers and basins in their rooms, and towels. Clint used his to clean up, then walked to the window to look out. He thought about Eclipse in Baton Rouge, and hoped the liveryman was looking after him.

There was a knock on his door, and then the door opened. Henri walked in.

"Is there gonna be any shootin' this time, boss?"

"I hope not," Clint said, "but I can't promise." He saw the disappointed look on his face. "Sorry," he said.

"I guess I'll just have to keep my head down."

"Henri, how bad could the flooding be in Baton Rouge?" Clint asked.

"Pretty bad," Henri said.

"How bad?"

"Things floating down the street, that bad."

"What kinds of things?"

"Lots of things," Henri said. "Barrels, buggies, bodies—"

"Bodies?"

"Dead bodies from the cemeteries," Henri said, "or people who have drowned. Sometimes you'll see the bodies of animals—dogs, cows, horses."

"Horses?"

"Yeah, why?"

"I left a horse back there, in one of the liveries."

"Oh, well, those guys are pretty good about caring for animals in their charge," Henri said. "They'll get them to high ground."

"They will?'

"If they have enough warning."

"How about out here?" Clint asked. "How would we have any warning?"

"We wouldn't, I guess," Henri said, "unless somebody came ridin' out, or Mr. Pivot got a telegraph message."

"The telegraph still works in a flood?"

"In a flood, yeah, I guess," Henri said. "The wires are up kinda high."

"What about in a storm like this?"

"More than likely," Henri admitted, "the wires would be down."

"Then how would Pivot have gotten a telegraph message about Baton Rouge being flooded?"

Henri shrugged and said, "He wouldn't."

"Damn it!" Clint said, heading for the door.

"What?" Henri asked.

"He lied to us!"

He was out the door before Henri got himself turned around to follow.

FORTY-SIX

Clint ran down the hall to the room Charles had put Cappy in, but when he burst in, she wasn't there. Henri came running in behind him.

"What's happening?"

"Pivot lied," Clint said. "Now he has Cappy somewhere. We have to find her."

"B-But where?"

"Downstairs. Come on."

They ran downstairs and the first thing they saw was water coming in from beneath the door.

"Oh, no," Henri said, pointing.

"I see it."

"The levee must have broken."

"How deep will it get?"

"There's no tellin'," Henri said. "It may take a boat to get out of the bayou."

"And this has happened before?"

"Yes."

"Why do people live here?"

Henri had no answer for that. Instead he said, "I'll have to release my horse so he can find higher ground."

"Okay, you do that," Clint said, "and I'll keep looking."

When Henri opened the door, more water gushed into the house.

"It's already knee deep," he called.

"Be careful," Clint said.

He started to search through the house, but all the rooms seemed empty. He stopped in the large living room and looked around. Where else could he search?

If Pivot was lying, then Cooper wasn't lying. That meant that he had worked for the man. Did that also mean he was telling the truth about Pivot having six men?

"Capucine!" he called out.

He heard something. A muffled sound, and then a thump.

"Cappy!"

More thumping.

"Keep it up," he yelled. "I'll find you."

The thumping continued until Clint reached the fireplace. He felt around it, and along the mantle, finally found a loose stone, and moved it. The fireplace moved, opened.

Behind it was a space just large enough to hold Cappy, who was tied to a chair. She'd barely had room to bang her feet against the back of the fireplace.

Clint pulled the chair out into the room and untied her.

"Who put you in there?"

"Jacques and his man, Charles."

"Just those two old men?"

She glared at him and said, "They had guns."

"And we still do, too."

Clint turned, saw Pivot and Charles standing in the doorway, each holding a gun.

"Where are your other men?" Clint asked.

"I have no other men," Pivot said. "Oh, Charles and I often use younger men to do our bidding, but apparently you killed the one I had watching Capucine."

"I didn't kill him," Clint said. "Keller did. And Cooper killed Keller."

"And Cooper?"

"I killed him," Capucine said, "and his wife."

"Too bad," Pivot said, "she was a lovely little Cajun."

"So now what?" Clint asked. "The water's rising outside, even as we speak."

"Charles and I know what to do," Pivot said. "We've been through this before."

"And us?"

"You'll drown in the flood."

"Why?"

The old man shrugged his bony shoulders.

"Why not?" he said. "Losing Capucine will cripple Devereaux."

"And me?"

"Wrong place, wrong time, Mr. Gunsmith," Pivot said. "Although I do get a thrill from knowing that I will be killing a legend."

"How do you propose to drown us?"

"Well, first you'll put her back in that chair. Then we'll find a chair for you."

"Really?" Clint asked. "The two of you will tie me to a chair?"

Charles suddenly looked a bit nervous, and the gun in his hand wavered.

"Drop your gun," Pivot said.

"If I take my gun from my holster, it will be to kill the two of you," Clint said. "Why would you have a man follow Capucine and never make a move?"

"He was supposed to make a move," Pivot said. "The fool fell in love with her. All he wanted to do was watch her."

Clint looked at Capucine, then back at Pivot.

"That happens to men," Clint said.

"Younger men," Pivot said. "Everything happens to younger men."

"Is that it?" Clint asked. "You hate younger men?"

"Why not?"

"It's not their fault," Clint said, "*our* fault, that we're young or that you're old."

"Drop your gun."

"I can't do that," Clint said, "and I can draw and fire before you pull the trigger. Believe me."

Clint could see that neither of these men was used to holding a gun. Neither of them had their finger on the trigger yet. But they had no younger men around to do the job for them.

"So? What do we do?" Clint asked.

"Shoot him," Pivot said.

Clint saw Charles move his finger to the trigger. Clint drew and fired. The old man crumbled to the floor. Pivot jumped, startled. He tried to pull the trigger of his gun, but his hand wouldn't cooperate.

Clint walked across the room and took the gun from the man's hand.

"Goddamn hands!" Pivot swore.

Henri came running in.

"The water's rising." He was wet to his torso.

Clint looked at Pivot.

"You said you and Charles have been through this before. How were you going to get out?"

"I hope you can swim," Pivot said peevishly. He walked to the sofa and sat down painfully.

"What do we do?" Capucine said. She was looking out the window. "It's rising fast."

"Pivot," Clint said, "is Baton Rouge really flooded?"

Pivot didn't answer. He was sitting on the sofa with his chin down on his chest.

"Is he asleep?" Cappy asked.

Clint walked to Pivot, touched his shoulder, then his back.

"No," he said, "he's dead."

"And so are we," Henri said.

"There must be a boat around here," Clint said. "That's the only way Pivot could have figured getting out."

"By the time we find it, the water could be over our heads," Cappy said.

"We have no choice," Clint said. "We have to start looking."

At that moment a window broke and water began to pour in. At the same time there was pounding on the front door.

"See who that is!" Clint snapped. "Cappy, see if those sofa cushions will float."

"You really think these will save us?"

"I don't know," Clint said. "I've never been through a flood before. Storms yes, but not floods."

"Boss," Henri said, rushing back, "you better look at this."

Henri led the way to the door, Clint and Cappy behind him. Outside they saw a rowboat floating, tied to one of the pillars.

"Who put that there?" Cappy asked.

"It doesn't matter," Clint said. "Let's get out of here!"

FORTY-SEVEN

Baton Rouge was not under water.

The levee had held; the city—and Eclipse—were safe. Clint discovered this when he, Cappy, and Henri returned from the bayou. The boat had taken them only so far, and when the water level receded, they got out and walked. By the time they got back, Capucine was happy to return to her house, with her husband.

"I've had enough excitement for one lifetime," she told Clint. She kissed his cheek and they said good-bye.

As for Henri, his cab was gone but his horse had found its way back to Baton Rouge. Clint decided to buy the young man a new cab. He felt he owed him that much.

Clint went to the livery to check Eclipse. He checked the horse over and the big Arabian was no worse for the wear. He thanked the liveryman and left the horse there for one more day.

He needed one night in his hotel to sleep in a bed and get some rest. He also wanted to think about the appearance of that boat outside Jacques Pivot's house. Somebody had tied off the boat, pounded on the door, and then beat a hasty retreat. Who had that person been? And how had they gotten away from the flood?

Whoever it was had saved his life.
Why?

The next day Clint left Baton Rouge on horseback, heading back to Texas. He'd had enough of Louisiana for a while. Hadn't even gotten to gamble. Maybe he should start thinking about himself after all these years and stop trying to help people. Yeah, right.

Behind Clint, and keeping out of sight for now, the man—*his* stalker—followed. Adams was lucky that he had followed him to the bayou and found that boat. The boat had been hidden in the woods next to a canoe. He tied the boat in front of the house for Adams and his companions, and had then taken himself to safety in the canoe. He had no idea who the boats belonged to, but whoever it was had pretty much saved them all from the flood.

The stalker decided to let Adams get to Texas before he closed the distance on him. Maybe, after following the Gunsmith for all these weeks, it was time to take the next step.

Watch for

THE SILENT DEPUTY

385th novel in the exciting GUNSMITH series
from Jove

Coming in January!

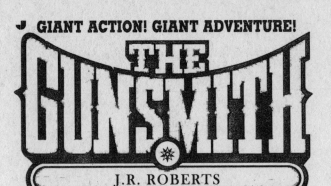

GIANT ACTION! GIANT ADVENTURE!

THE GUNSMITH

J.R. ROBERTS

Little Sureshot and
the Wild West Show
(Gunsmith Giant #9)

Dead Weight
(Gunsmith Giant #10)

Red Mountain
(Gunsmith Giant #11)

The Knights of Misery
(Gunsmith Giant #12)

The Marshal from Paris
(Gunsmith Giant #13)

Lincoln's Revenge
(Gunsmith Giant #14)

Andersonville Vengeance
(Gunsmith Giant #15)

The Further Adventures
of James Butler Hickok
(Gunsmith Giant #16)

penguin.com/actionwesterns

M455AS0812